"Do you really think we'll still be at the ranch on Christmas?" Nicole asked, and realized she wished they *would* be there.

Matt's eyes narrowed, and she wanted to reach up and press out the wrinkle above his nose, but she refrained from doing so.

"Even when this is all resolved, I don't want you to leave Lost Creek, but I don't really have anything to offer you." He ran a hand over the dark stubble on his jaw. "My life for the next few years is mapped out, and I can't change that."

Right. That again. She knew he didn't want a relationship, so why did hearing him say it cut her to the core?

She held up the key, eager to change the subject. "So... we should get going, right?"

He nodded but didn't look all that convinced. He gestured for her to precede him, and she took one last look at the Christmas tree before starting for the door.

It was suddenly kicked in.

Nicole screamed and lurched back as two men holding rifles burst inside.

"On the floor now!"

Susan Sleeman is a bestselling author of inspirational and clean-read romantic suspense books and mysteries. She received an RT Reviewers' Choice Best Book Award for *Thread of Suspicion. No Way Out* and *The Christmas Witness* were finalists for the Daphne du Maurier Award for Excellence. She's had the pleasure of living in nine states and currently lives in Oregon. To learn more about Susan, visit her website at susansleeman.com.

Books by Susan Sleeman

Love Inspired Suspense

McKade Law

Holiday Secrets
Rodeo Standoff
Christmas Hideout

First Responders

Silent Night Standoff
Explosive Alliance
High-Caliber Holiday
Emergency Response
Silent Sabotage
Christmas Conspiracy

The Justice Agency

Double Exposure
Dead Wrong
No Way Out
Thread of Suspicion
Dark Tide

Visit the Author Profile page at Harlequin.com for more titles.

CHRISTMAS HIDEOUT

SUSAN SLEEMAN

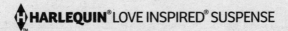
HARLEQUIN® LOVE INSPIRED® SUSPENSE

Recycling programs for this product may not exist in your area.

LOVE INSPIRED BOOKS

ISBN-13: 978-1-335-49073-5

Christmas Hideout

Copyright © 2018 by Susan Sleeman

www.Harlequin.com

Printed in U.S.A.

The Lord is nigh unto them that are of a broken heart...
—*Psalms* 34:18

A special thank-you to Susan Snodgrass
for naming Walt's horse, Thunderbolt; Julie Gilbert
for naming Jed's horse, Bullet; Lora Doncea for naming
Nicole's horse, Sunrise; and Debora Wilder
for naming Winnie's horse, Starlight.

ONE

The low, keening wail reverberated from the walls of Nicole Dyer's apartment as fear skittered through her body.

She listened. Hard. Trying to figure out where the sound originated.

Her. It was coming from her. She was the one crying out.

She clamped a hand over her mouth, stilling the noise before she woke her precious three-year-old daughter. Nicole stared at the warning message. Someone had laid a photo of her on the butcher-block countertop and plunged a large hunting knife into it.

The threat was clear. Someone wanted her dead. And that someone had to be the man she'd recently broken up with. Grady Harmon.

He'd finally lost it. Taken his obsession with her too far. They'd dated for months and all was good, but then he'd turned angry and controlling, and she'd dumped him before he could hurt her or sweet Emilie. But that didn't matter to him.

Not one bit.

Nicole had been receiving texts for a month from various phones and nothing could be tracked back to Grady, but she knew it had to be him. He'd constantly tried to keep her from doing anything without him, hounding her

and insisting he know her every move. So she'd ended
things with him, and he was angry about the breakup.
The messages started right after that, but soon changed
to threats on her life.

But this? This physical threat? The hunting knife?
This was too much.

How had he even gotten into her apartment?

Wait. Could he still be here?

She spun. Scanned the room, her heart racing.

Emilie. She had to protect Emilie.

Nicole grabbed the knife. Held it tight and raised it.
Armed now and prepared to save her child, she charged
down the hallway, fear stealing her breath. She shoved
open Emilie's door. Her sweet child lay in her bed. Curled
on her side. Her thumb firmly planted in her mouth.

Nicole sighed out her relief but didn't relax. She jerked
open the closet door. He wasn't there. She knelt to look
under the bed. Nothing.

She bolted for the door and checked her own bedroom. The closet. Under the bed. No intruder. She raced
to the hallway bathroom. Knife raised, she slid open the
shower curtain.

No Grady. No one.

A sigh of relief came to her lips, but she stifled it.
She couldn't relax. Not for a second. Not when he'd
stalked her. She saw him everywhere. At the grocery
store. Outside the school where she taught third grade.
At her church. He texted her. Demanded to get back together. Then started threatening her life. Daily. Sometimes hourly.

She'd reported everything to the police, but he used
an unregistered phone and they couldn't trace it. She'd
considered moving out of Austin to get away from him,
but she'd have to quit her job. Her husband had been a

great provider before he died, but he'd spent every penny he'd earned and left her with nothing. She had to work, and if she abandoned her job, how would she take care of Emilie?

And what would the point of moving be, anyway? Grady was a police officer, and he had ways to locate her anywhere. Especially here in Texas.

He'd even gotten into her apartment. He could come back at any time. Now. Tonight. Tomorrow. When she didn't know. Couldn't predict.

Panic raced along her nerves. She gulped for air. Couldn't find a breath. Panted. Tried harder. Looked for answers. For what to do.

She suddenly realized she was still clutching the knife and dropped it on the counter. The solid metal landed with a clang, ratcheting up her fear.

She needed help. Her sister. Piper. She'd call Piper. She was a voice of reason and could help Nicole think logically.

She grabbed her phone and dialed. "He's been here. Grady...in the apartment."

"Are you in danger?" Piper's urgent and worried question was nearly Nicole's undoing.

She took a breath and blew it out. Took another. "We're fine at the moment. He's gone, but he could come back."

"You need to call the police. Now!"

"What good will that do?"

"He violated his restraining order. They can lock him up, and all of this will be over."

Nicole snorted. "Like that's made a difference. I've called 911 on him so many times, and he's long gone before anyone arrives, so they think I'm crying wolf." Piper had to realize by now that as a cop, Grady knew how to play the game. To disappear as fast as he'd appeared. "I'll report him, but I can't rely on the cops to make sure he's punished for violating the order."

"Why did I ever date him?" An ache settled in Nicole's chest. "Him of all people to be the first guy to go out with since Troy died."

She hadn't dated in the three years since her husband had been killed in a motorcycle crash. She'd shut down for months, needing Piper just to get through her daily activities. But Nicole soon realized as a pregnant woman she had to find her footing again for the baby. To honor Troy and give their child the best chance in life. She started dating Grady after he came to her classroom to talk to her students. He was so compelling. So sweet with the kids, and she'd never been able to resist a guy who loved kids this way.

"You've got to quit beating yourself up about that," Piper said. "I still think you should call the police."

Nicole shot a look around her tiny apartment. "Grady wouldn't have touched anything without wearing gloves, and there's no sign of a forced entry."

"Then how did he get in?"

"I don't know. Maybe the windows." She ran to check the locks, window by window. "No, they're locked, and there's no sign he forced them open."

"What about the door?"

She raced to the front door. "No scratches or gouges from prying it open. He had to have a key."

"Did you give him one?"

"No. He insisted I have a key to his place, but I never gave him one for my apartment."

"Then how?"

"Maybe he used his status as a police officer to get the building manager to let him in. Yeah, that has to be it."

Piper sighed. "No matter what, you're not safe there. Come stay with me."

"No. No way. He'd find us at your place. I need to leave. To run." Nicole didn't need to think twice about her decision when Grady threatened to kill her, leaving Emilie an orphan.

Running was the answer.

The only answer.

But how and where?

She'd just have to play it by ear.

"I'll call you once we're safe." A thought burrowed into her brain. "No, wait. I can't take my phone. He can track it. I'll have to leave it here. I'll buy a prepaid phone the minute we're safe and call you."

She couldn't believe she was even thinking about running? Was it the right thing to do? Would they be safe?

"Honey, don't go," Piper pleaded, breaking Nicole's heart even more and raising her doubts. "Not like this. Not alone. I'll come—"

"I can't ask you to come along. I'll go to that cute bed-and-breakfast in the Texas Hill Country I stayed at with Troy. I'll call you the minute I get a new phone. I love you, sis." Nicole disconnected before she caved in.

She left the phone on the counter and raced to her room to jerk a tote bag from the closet. She needed clothes, sure, but she had to take items that were important to her, too. That gave her comfort. She didn't know when she would be back, *if* she would be back, and the journey would be tough. Nicole would ask Piper to pack the rest of their things and put them in storage.

She grabbed her mother's necklace. Her wedding ring. Her father's watch. Put them in the bag. She located Emilie's baby book and added it, too.

What next?

Should she even be doing this? Could she do it?

She looked at Emilie. Yes, for her, Nicole had to be strong.

She scanned the room. Pictures. She wanted to have family pictures with her. Piper's and their parents', who lived in Minnesota. This was the only way they could be with her to offer strength. She placed the frames into the bag. Next went her laptop and cords. Clothes followed. As many as she could fit in the bag.

She located a large backpack from her college days and hurried to Emilie's room to pack her belongings. She didn't want to risk Emilie dropping Mr. Monkey. Freeing him from her daughter's arms, she put him, then her favorite blanket and several changes of clothing, in the bag.

Bag zipped, Nicole surveyed Emilie's room. They'd just finished decorating the space with playful monkeys in bright colors that Emilie had chosen. She'd named each monkey and said good-night to them every night. Now she would have to leave them behind.

Tears pricked Nicole's eyes. She swiped them away. No time for tears when their safety was at risk. She slipped on the backpack and slung the tote bag over her shoulder.

Perfect. Nicole set off for the front door, passing the Christmas tree with Emilie's presents below. Only a week away, and Nicole was ready for the usual celebration with Piper. Now Emilie wouldn't have a family Christmas.

Tears flooded Nicole's eyes. Sobs followed, her body convulsing.

No. Stop. You have to keep it together for Emilie. Go! Now!

She breathed deeply, willed her tears away to pack food and her own personal items. She shrugged the bags over her shoulder and returned to pick Emilie up. She held her daughter close, inhaling the sweet scent of her shampoo. In the foyer, Nicole snatched her keys from the table where she'd left them when she'd come home from an extended day at work to find the knife. *Home*. Not home any longer. Not since she'd spotted the knife.

She fumbled through the key ring to grasp the fob for her car. She held it at the ready. The moment she got in range of her car, she would press the button and unlock the doors. She wouldn't lock the dead bolt. No time for that. She'd have Piper take care of that, too.

At the door, Nicole pressed her ear against the cool metal and listened. She'd wait to step out until she heard people outside. Grady wouldn't likely approach when others were around and could act as witnesses to his visit. Sure, he would still try to follow her, but if he did, she had to hope she could lose him.

The moment she heard voices, she opened the door. Took a deep breath and mentally prepared to run for her car.

She pressed the button on the key fob. Heard the resulting beeps.

"This is it, baby," Nicole whispered to her still-sleeping child.

She took off. Moving at top speed through the freezing night air. She reached her car. Jerked open the back door and settled Emilie. Nicole hated having her back exposed, but she had no choice. She couldn't take off without Emilie safely buckled in her car seat.

Trembling hands made Nicole clumsy with the straps. "C'mon. C'mon. C'mon. Faster."

She clicked the last one. Ripped the tote from her shoulder. Tossed it inside the car. Did the same with the backpacks and hopped into the front seat. She locked the door and got the car started.

She looked around. Searching. Scanning. Trying to find Grady.

She didn't spot him. His truck. It made sense that he thought she'd call the police about the knife, and he'd already taken off.

She backed the car out and headed for the exit. She merged onto the street and pointed the car toward the freeway.

Yes! They were going to make it. Going to get away.

First stop would be the ATM for cash.

Wait. Cash.

No, oh, no.

She'd left her purse behind. She'd dropped it on the floor when they'd come home, and she'd carried Emilie to her bed. Nicole had no wallet. No ID. No ATM card. No credit card. Not that she'd use one of those, as Grady could track the purchases, but she had to get cash somehow.

She would have to go back. Take Emilie from the car. Race in and grab the purse and race out again. It would be okay. She hadn't seen Grady in the lot, and it should be safe.

She made a U-turn. Entered the parking lot again. Glanced around. Her gaze locked on a pickup truck. A gray one. Like Grady's.

She searched the cab.

A man sat there.

He turned.

Smiled.

Locked gazes.

Grady.

No, oh, no. Why did it have to be him?

She shifted into Reverse and tore out of the lot, hop-

ing with every fiber of her being that she could lose him
before he found a way to stop them and inflict any harm.

An intruder?

Deputy Matt McKade parked his patrol car out of
view of the cabin, his warning senses tingling. The cabin
was located on his family's dude ranch in the Texas Hill
Country. He'd grown up at Trails End but now lived in
an apartment in Lost Creek, just a few miles away, as
did all of his siblings. But his parents and grandparents
still lived in the main house. Matt and his three siblings
also spent a lot of time there.

His parents and grandparents were out of town, and
he'd promised to check in on the cabins while they were
gone. Just two days, and they'd taken a break from rent-
ing cabins during the holidays and had no guests. He
simply had to make a morning and evening inspection
to be sure things were fine. No biggie, right?

Yeah, right. Until now. He'd just arrived for his evening inspection and found lights glowing in one of the
cabins.

Could be a vagrant squatting again. They'd had problems with that in the past, hence the morning and evening checks. But it could be more than that, too. Vagrant
or not, as a deputy, there was no way he would approach
without taking precautions. Starting with killing his
headlights and parking out of sight.

He climbed out of his vehicle and closed his door with
a quiet click that seemed to reverberate through the frosty
December night. He lifted his sidearm and approached
the small building, the last cabin in a neat row of six. Located nearest to the main road, it was the building that
vagrants seemed to favor when it was vacant.

He moved ahead, his breath whispering out in tiny

white clouds. He passed the dude ranch's large fire pit. The horseshoe pit. The tall, bald cypress with a tire swing, all items favored by their guests. One step, then another. Making sure to move slowly to keep his feet from crunching on fallen leaves and alerting the intruder inside.

He approached the side window, the light growing brighter as he walked. He glanced inside. Spotted someone sitting on the sofa, the small lamp illuminating their head tilted at an angle. He watched. They didn't move. Not a fraction of an inch. Asleep or dead, he didn't know.

Warning bells clanged in his brain.

If the person was asleep, his best bet was to make a surprise entry. He took out his master key and went to the door. A quick turn of the lock and knob, then a push, and he had the door open. He flipped on the overhead light.

"Police," he shouted, using the universal name that all law enforcement used regardless of their agency affiliations when approaching a potentially dangerous person. "Don't move."

The person startled. Sat forward.

What in the world?

A young woman holding a child stared at him, her eyes wide, terror etched in the depths.

"I'm sorry." She blinked against the bright light. "I know I shouldn't be here. My car. It broke down. We were so tired and cold. I didn't have blankets for my daughter. She'd freeze. I got the window open, and we came in. I…I'm sorry. Please don't arrest me, Officer…"

"Deputy McKade. Matt McKade." He blew out his adrenaline on a long wave of air, his mind trying to calm down and figure out how to handle this intruder. He'd start by identifying her. "What's your name?"

"Nicole. Nicole Dyer." She peered down on the child.

"This's my daughter, Emilie. We live in Austin. I'm a widow and my ex-boyfriend has been stalking me. At first, I thought he was just trying to intimidate me into getting back together with him. But he's gotten progressively angrier and threatening. Tonight, he left a knife in my kitchen. He's threatened to kill me. So I ran, but I left my purse at home and don't have any money. I'd only driven an hour or so when my car broke down and I had nowhere to go." Her words rolled over each other like tumbleweeds in a dust storm on the open Texas range.

Matt didn't like hearing of a stalker. Didn't like it one bit. Stalkers were often all talk and no action, but this guy, if she could be believed, sounded like the deadly type, and she was right to fear for her life.

But could she be believed? His first instinct was to trust her. She seemed too upset to be making this up. Didn't matter. He was a sworn officer of the law, and he couldn't just take her word for it. "Do you have any identification?"

She shook her head and bit her full bottom lip. It was then that he allowed himself to take a good look at her. She had big icy-blue eyes still wide with fear. High cheeks. Wavy blond hair pulled back into a bun, but strands had fallen free and lay softly against her creamy skin. In a word, beautiful, and something about her got to him in a way he hadn't felt in a long time.

Before he communicated his attraction, he forced his gaze from her face and it landed on the child all snuggled up to her mother. She had blond curls and an angelic face that people must fawn over.

"Are you arresting me?" Nicole met his gaze and locked on.

Her vulnerability pulled at him, triggering something deep inside. She broke into the cabin, had a story to tell and he what? He simply believed her story because she was pretty?

Right. He could just hear his sheriff father lecturing him about this kind of behavior. Matt had a job to do here. To figure out if she was telling the truth. But he clearly didn't need to keep his weapon out.

He holstered it. "Do you know your car's license plate number?"

"Yes! Yes! Perfect. You can check that out, can't you?" She flashed a quick smile—her way of saying thanks, he supposed—and rattled off the numbers. "It's a Honda Accord. White. 1996."

"Registered in Texas?"

She nodded.

"And what's your date of birth?" he asked, now easily sliding into his deputy role.

She quickly provided the information, and he didn't even have to calculate her age. They were born the same year, making her thirty-two.

He inserted the earbud for his radio in his ear. In his mic, he repeated the information she'd provided and requested a DMV lookup, along with information from the associated driver's license and details of the restraining order. If he was in his car, he could handle all of this himself, including seeing her photo on her driver's license, but he wouldn't leave her here and go back to his car.

While he waited for dispatch to retrieve the information, he turned his attention back to Nicole. "Tell me about the warning you received tonight."

She took a deep breath and shifted to face him. "He left a big knife—a foot long and like the ones I know he uses for hunting. He stabbed it into a picture of me on my countertop made of butcher block. No written message. Just that horrible, horrible terrifying visual message while Emilie was sleeping in the next room. I panicked. Packed our bags, grabbed Emilie and fled." She flashed her gaze filled with shock and disbelief up to his.

Whatever had happened had affected her deeply. Despite his desire to remain impartial, his protective instinct rose up. He tried to tamp it down. It was awful early in their conversation to believe she needed protection of any sort, but even a hint of a woman in physical danger riled him to no end, and he couldn't just push it away.

"Did you call the police?" he asked.

She shook her head and lifted her chin in a defiant tilt. "What good would it do? I called so many times in the past, and they didn't help. His name is Grady Harmon. He's a police officer, and by the time his fellow cops show up, he's long gone, and they don't believe me."

Say what? The guy was a law enforcement officer? That put a different spin on things.

Matt didn't automatically assume all cops were good people. They weren't, just like anyone in any other profession, but whether or not he was good, officers initially took the side of one of their brothers until facts proved otherwise. Might not be the right response, but they needed to depend on their fellow officers having their backs. Sometimes they took it too far, though, and protected their own when they didn't deserve it.

She sighed. "You'd think they'd realize I had to have proof of his actions to get the restraining order, but they don't seem to take that into account."

"I'm not saying you don't have proof, but I do know that judges these days will most always side with the victim. Officers know this and can be skeptical."

"You, too, I see." Her eyes darkened to the shade of a new pair of Wranglers, and she glared at him.

Even with her tense expression, she touched something inside him, and he wanted to help her. "I'm not saying they're right or wrong. I'm just saying the burden of proof for a restraining order is lighter than most legal proceedings."

"He really has been stalking me." She raised her shoulders into a hard line. "I don't lie. It goes against my Christian beliefs."

She was a Christian. Of course, anyone could claim to be a believer. And believers lied at times, too. Matt knew that from his job. People lied to officers all the time. People he saw in church on Sunday.

Sure, he wanted to take her word at face value—wanted to believe her, but even if he wanted to, he couldn't. He was a deputy, and that meant checking facts and living by those facts. Not the word of a woman who piqued his interest. Actually, just the opposite.

Because he was attracted to her, he would do even more digging before buying into her story. Still, she could be assured if there was any hint of danger, he'd step up and make sure they were safe. No way he'd leave them to the mercies of a dangerous stalker. No way.

TWO

Nicole had never grilled a steak, but she felt like a burnt and crispy slab of meat after this deputy's many questions. He stood there staring at her. Matt McKade, he'd said. One hand on a trim waist. One resting on the butt of his gun. A power play? Maybe. Or was he used to relaxing his hand that way? Grady had often done that.

Still, when Matt glanced at Emilie, she caught a hint of compassion in eyes that had burrowed right through her. To be fair to him, she *had* broken the law, but she had no choice. Okay fine, she might have stayed in the car, but it was just too cold for Emilie, and Nicole wasn't prepared with warm blankets. She'd searched for nearby houses with lights on, but she'd seen nothing. Then she spotted the Trails End dude ranch sign and the line of empty rental cabins. For her daughter's sake, she'd wiggled the window hard until the catch gave way and she could creep inside. As she told the deputy, she felt bad for doing so and never would have broken in if Emilie's life wasn't in jeopardy. She wouldn't apologize or defend herself again. Either this guy believed her, or he didn't. She'd just have to wait for his verdict.

He jerked his head away and shook it. Why, she had no idea.

"Back to when you reported violations of the restraining order," he suddenly said. "Are you getting a lack of cooperation from everyone in the department?"

She took a breath and warned herself to be patient and not snap at him when he was just doing his job. "I've only interacted with the responding officers. I have no idea who else in his department even knows about this."

Emilie stirred in Nicole's arms. Guilt was eating at Nicole for putting her child in this precarious situation, so she started rocking to keep her daughter from waking. How could she have done this to Emilie? Tears burned the back of Nicole's eyes, but she fought hard against them. Emilie needed her to stay strong and fix this, not blubber like a baby.

She met Matt's gaze, and even when his eyes held a challenge, she didn't look away. "One thing I do know is I can't count on the police. I have to take care of myself and Emilie. I've heard stories about women dying at the hands of their stalkers. I won't let that happen to me or my child."

He ground his teeth for a moment. "You're right, it does happen. Catching a stalker can often take a long time. That's even truer of an officer. Like you said, he knows how the system works and can game it."

"Exactly." Hope blossomed that he might believe her.

He glanced at Emilie. "How old is your daughter?"

"She just turned three. I was eight months pregnant with her when my husband, Troy, died. His motorcycle was hit by a car."

The deputy suddenly pressed his finger against his earbud and tipped his head as if listening. "I'm away from my computer and need a physical description from the DL."

Nicole assumed he meant "driver's license," as that

was the only thing the police would have with her physical description.

He ran his gaze over her from head to toe, lingering for a long time on her face, before he stared over her shoulder.

Was he checking to see if she matched that description? Likely. She didn't like that he wouldn't take her word on her ID, but she also knew from her time with Grady that people frequently lied to law enforcement officers, and with their very lives at stake all the time, they couldn't be too cautious.

"And the RO in effect?" He listened to the answer, his forehead narrowing. "Any crimes involved causing an action to be taken on behalf of the RO?"

He might be speaking law enforcement lingo, but she got that he was asking if Grady had violated the restraining order. The deputy wouldn't ask if he believed her, but so what? They would tell him about the number of times she'd called, and he'd know she was telling the truth.

"Pull up Harmon's DMV details and email them to me." He released his finger, and his narrowed gaze landed on her again.

"Are you convinced of my identity?" she asked.

"Yes," he said. "And I've also confirmed the restraining order, but there's no record of Harmon violating it or the police response."

"What?" she shouted, and Emilie stirred. Nicole rocked harder to keep her daughter from waking. "He's violated it tons of times, and the police responded each time. I kept a record of it, but it's at my apartment."

"Relax." He held up a hand. "Because they didn't arrest Harmon, the official reports won't show their response."

"They didn't keep a record? How can that be?"

"They have a record. It's just recorded on their blotter instead of in the official arrest system. Blotter records will show that they responded to your residence and the results of their response. Unfortunately, though, these aren't readily available to outside agencies."

"But you will request them, right? So you know I'm telling the truth."

He gave a clipped nod. "Do you have any reason to believe Harmon would know your whereabouts right now?"

"Would he?" Panic flared. "No…no…he didn't follow us. I made sure of that. He couldn't, right?"

"He *is* a police officer and would know how to tail you without you being aware of it."

"Oh, no…yes, he could. He was in the parking lot and saw me leave."

"What about your phone? Is it turned on?"

"No…no. I was worried he could trace it, so I left it in the apartment. With the car breaking down, I'm not sure that was a good decision. I planned to buy a new phone, but I don't have money. I can call my sister in the morning. She'll bring my wallet to me, and I can get that phone and also pay for the cabin."

"No." He fired her a sharp warning look. "That's not a good idea."

Her heartbeat shot up. "Why not?"

"If what you say about Harmon is true, he could be watching your apartment, and she could lead him here."

"Yes, right. Yes. I can totally see him doing that. But what do I do? I need money to fix my car. To pay for this cabin." Her heart sank. "What have I done taking off like that? I shouldn't have been so hasty. But Emilie… I had to protect her. I just had to."

The deputy took a step closer. "We can work all of that out in the morning. For now, let's solve the immediate problem of where you'll spend the night. You can't stay here. I—"

"I know," she interrupted. "We're trespassing. The owners will be angry. I'll get our things, and we'll leave." She started to rise.

He held up his hand, his eyes narrowing into a hard look that gave her a moment's pause, and she didn't dare move another muscle.

"That's not what I meant," he said.

Oh, right! She'd misunderstood, but now she got it. "You're going to arrest me…aren't you?" Thoughts zinged through her brain. "What about Emilie? What will happen to her? I don't…no…I…"

"No, wait. Let me explain." He flashed up his hand again. "I'm not arresting you, and I'm not tossing you out into the cold. My family owns this ranch, and they're out of town, so I'm housesitting for them. I won't leave you in the cabin. Not alone. Harmon could have followed you, and you aren't safe. I'd like you to stay up at the main house."

"With you?"

"I'm not a threat."

"No offense, but I didn't think Grady was a threat, either, and look where I am now." If her arms had been free, she would cross them to tell him she meant business.

He looked like he wanted to sigh but didn't. "You and Emilie can stay on the second floor, and I'll sleep on the first floor. The house was built in the 1800s. The stairs creak something fierce, and you'll hear anyone who tries to come up the staircase."

"I don't—"

That sigh he'd been fighting finally came pouring out. "The way I see it, you only have two other options— sleep in your car while I park my vehicle next to you, or

I stay in this small cabin with you. Whatever your decision, I won't leave you to fend for yourself when you could be in danger." His tone had taken on a life of its own, fierce and to the point, but instead of scaring her, she believed it meant if danger lurked he'd be right there fighting it back. Grady had often tried to manage her the same way, but this deputy's caring tone said he had her best interest at heart, where Grady had just seemed to want his own way.

"We'll stay at the house," she said and got up with Emilie.

She only hoped this man—this big, towering deputy, a fierce defender of the downtrodden if she could believe him—was the man he claimed to be, and she wasn't making a big mistake that could cost her or Emilie dearly. After all, she'd trusted Grady and that didn't work out well for them. Not well at all.

The next morning, something tickled Matt's nose, and he shifted on the couch to brush it off. A giggle came from beside him as he attempted to go back to sleep. He flashed his eyes open and met the very big blue eyes of Nicole's daughter gazing at him, an impish grin on her face as she brushed the tail of a stuffed monkey against his nose. Morning sun streamed through the ranch house's picture window behind her, giving her feathery blond hair a soft halo.

"Hi," she said, her voice squeaky and high.

"Hi." He blinked hard to try to come fully alert after being awake most of the night worrying about this munchkin and her mother. He didn't much like the fact that he'd been sleeping hard enough not to hear this tiny imp come down the stairs. He had to do a better job of staying alert for this little family.

He smiled at her. "I'm Matt, and you must be Emilie."

"Uh-huh." She gave him a shy smile.

"Where's your mother?"

"In bed."

"Does she know you're down here?"

"Nuh-uh."

"Do you think we should tell her?"

"She's sleeping. Don't want to wake her up." She bit her lower lip for a moment. "I'm hungry."

Matt glanced at the large grandfather clock. It had been in his family for generations, sitting on the mantel. Wow, it was eight already. The only time he slept this late was when he worked the graveyard shift, but after he'd gotten Nicole and Emilie settled in a guest room upstairs, he'd tossed and turned on the sofa until the wee hours of the morning. The stern face of Grady Harmon as seen on his driver's license kept invading Matt's thoughts. Matt had done a basic background check on Harmon before he'd gone to sleep last night. The guy had so many advantages as a police officer and knew how to work the system. He also knew how criminals thought and could emulate them when it came to stalking Nicole.

The very thought left Matt unsettled and worried. He still felt that way and would follow up on that blotter information for Harmon's restraining order to discover if Nicole's story was true.

He swung his feet to the floor. "Do you like chocolate chip pancakes?"

"Yummy."

"Then follow me to the kitchen, and I'll make a batch." He stood and stepped into the foyer.

Emilie stopped near a ten-foot Christmas tree covered in family heirloom ornaments. The pine scent filled the space.

She stared up at it. "I like your Christmas tree."

"Me, too. My mom and nana decorate it every year. Some of these ornaments are as old as my granddad."

Her eyes widened in appreciation.

Matt pointed at a varnished dough snowman. "My nana made each of us a snowman with our names and birthdates. This one is mine."

"I want one with my name, too."

"I'm sure if you asked Nana when she gets home today she'll make one for you."

"Goody." She danced with joy and her blond curls sprang into action.

"Let's get those pancakes." He led the way to the farm-style kitchen.

On the near side of the room sat a big breakfast table where he'd joined his family more times than he could begin to count. He pulled a chair out for Emilie. She climbed up. The chair seemed monster-sized when her tiny body settled in the middle of the worn wooden seat. She'd never be able to eat by sitting in the chair. What in the world did he do to solve that? Hopefully her mother would've gotten up by then. She'd know what to do.

He grabbed orange juice, eggs and milk from the well-stocked refrigerator. His nana did all the cooking for the family, and since he and his three siblings showed up for lunch or dinner on a regular basis, she always kept it filled with food.

He faced Emilie. "Would you like some orange juice?"

"Yes, please." She smiled up at him. Such sweetness and innocence.

His heart melted into a big old puddle. Smiling, he dug in the cupboard and found a red plastic Kool-Aid cup with a big smile etched on the side that he'd had as a kid and poured her a glass. He placed the cup on the table in front of her.

"Thank you," she said.

She was a polite little thing. He had to give her mother props for that.

She traced her finger over the Kool-Aid man's face and giggled. "He's smiling."

Matt chuckled with her and got lost in the sound of her pure joy. Law enforcement officers could develop jaded opinions. He was no exception, he supposed. To see pure happiness over such a simple thing was refreshing.

She took a long drink, and he turned back to the cupboards to retrieve pancake ingredients, plus a bowl and whisk, and started mixing. *That* he knew how to do. Taking care of a three-year-old? Not so much. Sure, he'd had training for his job on how to handle people of all ages but caring for a child like this was another thing all together.

He always imagined he would have his own kids someday and would learn as he went along, but he'd never dated anyone he wanted to settle down with. But this was a crash course in figuring it out, and his confidence was nearly absent. Left him unsettled.

His phone rang. Seeing it was from his sister Kendall, also a Lake County deputy, he quickly accepted the call.

"Sis," he said.

"I followed up on the Austin PD blotter like you asked me last night."

"And?" he asked, not liking her reserved tone.

"The desk sergeant said he'd work on gathering the information when he had time."

"You told him this was urgent, right?"

"Of course." She sounded like she didn't appreciate him following up on her. "But he said he'd get to it when he got to it."

"Translated, it will take a while."

"And if the sarge is Harmon's buddy, it'll take longer."

Matt heard Emilie's bare feet padding across the room to the low window, and he turned to look at her.

"You've got to keep after them," he said, putting as much force into his tone as possible. "Lives could depend on us getting the information."

"Don't worry. I've got it."

Right, don't worry. How could he not? He shoved his phone into his pocket. The adorable child and her mother could be in danger, and he needed information and needed it now.

"Horsies! You have horsies!" Emilie swung around to face him. Her eyes, alive with delight, reminded him of her mother's.

"Can I ride a horsey?" Emilie shoved her monkey under one arm and tucked it by her side.

"Sure," Matt quickly replied but instantly thought better of his hasty response. "If your mother says it's okay, that is."

Emilie's forehead furrowed, and her lips puckered in an adorable pout that he thought would make it nearly impossible to say no to anything she asked for. How could such a bitty child have such power over an adult? He'd never experienced anything like it.

"Mommy doesn't like horses," she said. "She's scared of them."

"Is that so?" Maybe while Nicole was staying at the ranch, he could help her get over that fear. After all, he wouldn't mind spending time with such a beautiful woman, but forming an attachment to either of them was out of the question. He needed to keep his focus on his work only and personal relationships were off-limits for him.

"She'll say no." Emilie's pout grew more exaggerated.

"I'll talk to her about it. Maybe I can convince her it's safe."

"Goody." She clapped her hands and turned her attention back to the window.

He started on the pancakes, and while they were cooking, he laid three place settings at the table in case Nicole woke up.

When he'd plated the last pancake, he took them to the table along with a bottle of rich maple syrup. "Pancakes are ready."

"Yippee." Emilie skipped across the room, but when she reached the chair her lips dipped in a monster-sized frown. "I need my booster seat."

That she did, and he still didn't know how to help her. Here he was a deputy who could face just about anything, and he was thrown by handling a tiny little girl with a smile that melted his heart and a pout that made him want to fix everything on the spot. Most importantly, it made him want to do everything he could to protect her from their stalker. After he confirmed Harmon had indeed been stalking them.

"Mommy lets me sit on her lap when we don't have my booster."

Right. Lap. "Would you like to sit on my lap?"

"Yes, please."

"What about your monkey? We don't want him to get all sticky, do we?"

She frowned and crossed her arms. "I want to sit with Mr. Monkey."

"But your mom wouldn't appreciate a sticky monkey," he said, grasping at straws for an answer.

Her expression didn't change.

Panic assailed him, and he never panicked. What did he say to a child who hadn't developed reasoning skills yet?

"If you want to eat, you can't hold on to Mr. Monkey." There, he'd stated it plainly but still held his breath as he waited for her response.

"Mr. Monkey can sit in his own chair." She placed him on a nearby chair and pushed it in. "He likes pancakes, too."

Matt sat, and she slipped up onto his lap. She didn't sit still for even a second but wiggled around until she was comfortable. "You haveta cut my pancakes."

Matt used his fork to slice them into small bites, but she kept squirming, and he had to constantly shift around her. How could a simple act of cutting up food be so difficult?

"I like syrup." She picked up the fork, and it looked as big as a pitchfork in her miniature hand.

He poured the syrup, and she attacked the pancakes as if she hadn't eaten in weeks. He reached for his own bite and she bumped the fork on his hand. He licked the sticky syrup off, but his attention soon shifted to the dripping bite she dropped on his jeans.

Were kids always this messy? If so how did he handle it? Ignore it and deal with the mess at the end, maybe?

Yeah, he'd keep his thoughts on the blotter information, and then when she was finished eating, he might have to hose them both off.

So what did he do about the information Kendall just relayed? With Harmon being an officer, Matt had to be smart about it. He could call one of his contacts higher up on the Austin police force to get the ball rolling. No, if he did that, word was more likely to get back to Harmon that someone in Lost Creek was inquiring about the RO.

He wouldn't make that call just yet. He'd give the department until the end of the day to provide the report. If they didn't, he'd have Kendall reach out. A casual follow-up by her shouldn't alert the desk sergeant into thinking the request was a big deal.

After all, the last thing Matt wanted to do was have this sergeant run to Harmon about the request and give away Nicole and Emilie's location to the potentially deadly stalker.

THREE

Hearing Emilie's giggle coming from the kitchen, the deputy's—Matt as he'd told her to call him last night—chuckle deep and rumbly, Nicole sagged against the door and sighed out her fear. When she'd woken up to find Emilie missing, she'd been certain Grady had somehow found them and gotten to her daughter to take her as a bargaining chip. He'd never threatened Emilie, but after seeing the knife last night, Nicole had no idea what horrific things Grady was capable of doing.

Their laughter died off. A long silence followed.

"What's wrong?" Matt asked, his voice laced with concern.

"I miss Mommy. But she needs to keep sleeping. She's tired because we had to go away from Grady. He wants to hurt Mommy."

"Did she tell you that?" Matt's tone held surprise.

"Nuh-uh. I heard her talking to Aunt Piper."

Oh, Emilie. I thought you were sleeping. Baby, I'm so sorry.

Nicole had been so careful not to let Emilie know what was going on with Grady, and until this, she'd succeeded because Emilie still had thought Grady was a good guy and wondered why he didn't visit them anymore.

"Don't worry, princess," Matt replied, his tone restrained. "I'm a deputy. Do you know what that is?"

"Police."

"Sheriff's department, and I won't let anything bad happen to your mommy. Not today. Not ever." The vehemence in his tone cut clear through Nicole, and she could hardly believe she'd happened upon a cabin with a deputy who cared enough to come to their rescue.

He seemed like such a good guy on the surface, and she wanted to believe he meant what he said. But at first Grady had doted on Emilie, and he'd promised to care for them, too. Look what happened with him. And now, thanks to Nicole letting him in their life, she would need to have a difficult discussion with her three-year-old, who was way too young to hear about bad people like Grady in the world.

Oh, God, why? How could You let this happen?

Okay, fine. God wasn't responsible. She was.

Here she was, blaming Him when she needed His guidance. She'd known what she was doing when she'd said yes to Grady. Sure, just because he wasn't a man of faith it didn't in any way mean he'd turn out to be a stalker, but she'd known about God's warning in the Bible not to yoke herself to an unbeliever. She'd ignored that and followed her attraction to Grady. She'd made her own trouble and needed to work it out on her own. Only then could she feel good about resuming her relationship with God.

For now, she'd stay strong. For herself. For Emilie. And not trust in another man, even a man like Matt, who seemed like a good guy.

She drew in a breath of air and stepped into the kitchen, where bright aqua cabinets greeted her like sunshine on a cloudy day. The countertops were well-worn and held a big white farm sink. Gingham curtains hung on a large window. The room looked like a kitchen from the past, when times were simpler and families gathered every day around worn farm tables like this one.

Emilie sat on Matt's lap, stabbing a fork into chocolate chip pancakes. So the guy could cook, and he took the time to make breakfast for Emilie. That one thoughtful act drew her to his side, and she knew she had to guard against that. And guard against how she was responding to the picture the two of them made.

Emilie looked so small next to his broad shoulders and muscular arm wrapped around her waist. A surprising sense of peace flooded Nicole, and she swallowed hard to keep from forgetting her vow of a moment ago not to let this man sway her good sense.

Emilie looked up and smiled, and Matt's lips tipped in a wide grin, too. He really seemed to be enjoying his time with Emilie. The scene was so precious to Nicole. A scene she'd often imagined after Troy passed away. He was such a caring and compassionate man and would have been a good father. A wonderful one, in fact.

What kind of father would Matt be? If this scene was any indication, a good one.

See, those are the kinds of thoughts you need to stop thinking.

"Hi, Mommy," Emilie said but didn't hop down for a hug the way she normally would.

Her daughter was very outgoing and precocious. Nicole wasn't at all surprised that she'd come downstairs and seemed to be having a good time with Matt but she didn't much like that Emilie had been so trusting.

"Matt made pancakes," she gushed as if it was the most awesome thing in the world. "And he said we could ride horsies if you said it was okay. Is it okay, Mommy? Is it?"

Nicole didn't appreciate being the one who had to say no.

"I'm sorry," he said as if reading her mind. "She said you were afraid of horses, and I didn't want your fear to keep her from riding."

Great. So he thought she was putting her desires first, and she was a bad mother on top of everything else. That would make it far easier to ignore her attraction to him.

She stepped over to the table and dropped onto a chair to look at Emilie. "We won't be here long enough for you to ride."

"You're not planning to leave, are you?" Matt asked. "Not with...you know."

"We'll be going once my car is fixed, and I figure out a way to pay for it and the cabin for last night. Hopefully that can happen today."

He frowned. "If what you told me last night is true, I don't like the thought of you two driving off unprotected."

Right. If what she said was true. He still didn't believe her.

Was it because Grady was a cop, or because Matt just wouldn't believe anyone until checking them out? Though she'd learned that law enforcement officers had suspicious personalities, she'd foolishly hoped Matt would've thought about this overnight and would've realized she was sincere. Not that it mattered if she was leaving today, but she still didn't want him to think she was a liar.

"What's *unprotected* mean?" Emilie asked around a mouthful of pancakes.

"Never mind, honey." When Emilie turned her attention back to her pancakes, Nicole slashed a hand across her throat to tell Matt any additional discussion of Grady was forbidden.

His frown deepened but then cleared, as if he had iron will to change his emotions in a moment. The same way Grady could change, too. Like a chameleon. She lifted her shoulders and prepared for a different personality to appear.

"The first thing we should do is get your car towed into the local garage," Matt said. "If it would help, I'm glad to call them while you eat breakfast."

Okay, so the same guy. Kind and considerate. Could she trust that? Did she want to trust it when it could be the first step in buying into a facade to gain her cooperation?

Seriously, she was such a hypocrite. She wanted him to trust her, but she wasn't willing to trust him. But she had Emilie to think about. She opened her mouth to say she could make the arrangements, but a local deputy would likely have some pull with the garage and might get her car looked at today.

She forced out a smile. "I'd appreciate you calling the garage. And I appreciate you making breakfast for Emilie. That was very kind of you."

"No biggie. Gave me an excuse to have one of the favorite breakfasts my nana used to make. Though I have to say, I didn't make them heart-shaped like hers." A wide, sincere smile crossed his face, and her heart picked up speed.

She'd been too worried and afraid last night to get more than an initial impression of him, but in the light of day, there was no avoiding the fact that he was not only a good-looking guy, but also heart-stoppingly handsome. His face was angular, all etched and chiseled. His hair was almost as dark brown as his eyes had been last night, but now as he smiled, his eyes were liquid like melted chocolate. And his smile. Wow. He had a way of making her feel like it was just for her, and he'd never share it with anyone else.

Powerful. So powerful. Drawing emotions out that Grady never raised, and she'd thought she'd buried with Troy.

The sound of the front door opening broke through her thoughts.

Grady.

She spun in her chair, her heart racing. She soon heard voices.

"That'll be my parents and grandparents," Matt said.

Nicole almost sagged in relief.

"What's that I smell coming from the kitchen?" a male voice boomed. "You make pancakes, Matt?"

"Matt never cooks," a woman said. "You're likely smelling some leftovers he heated in the microwave."

Footsteps coming toward the kitchen followed the comments. Nicole ran a hand through her hair in preparation of meeting Matt's family. She'd raced out of the bedroom in search of Emilie and was still wearing her pajamas. Once she'd discovered that Emilie was fine, she should have thought to go up and change, but she'd been too shocked by hearing Emilie announce that she knew about Grady to remember her pajamas.

"Well, well, well," an older gentleman with a thick head of gray—almost white—hair said. "What do we have here?"

A woman—his wife, Nicole presumed—stepped up behind him and peered at Nicole. "What's going on?"

Another man and woman entered the room. Matt was a spitting image of the second man, only younger. Trim, the second man wore a Western shirt and jeans with a thick belt. The woman, whom Nicole guessed to be in her fifties or early sixties, was tall and slender with blond hair pulled back in a ponytail.

"Everyone, this is Nicole and her daughter, Emilie," Matt said.

"Hi." Nicole could only come up with one word as the others studied her with extreme interest.

"Walt McKade, Matt's father." The younger man held out his hand.

As they shook hands, Walt introduced his wife, Winnie; mother, Betty; and father, Jed. The others smiled their welcome, but the smiles were reserved and tight.

"What's going on, Matt?" Winnie asked.

"Why don't we leave Nicole and Emilie to finish their breakfasts, and I'll update you in the family room?" Matt didn't wait for a response but settled Emilie on Nicole's lap and shooed his family toward the door.

Was he embarrassed to be seen with them? Caught with her in her pajamas? Of course he was. She'd invaded his life, and now his family was taken aback. She just kept doing the wrong thing since she'd met him. Even more reason to get that car fixed and take off.

When Matt reached the doorway, Nicole grabbed his wrist to stop him and peered up at him. "I'm so sorry for intruding this way."

"Hey." He smiled, that sweet one that made her heart yearn for more. "You're welcome here at the ranch for as long as you need to stay. Once I explain the situation, my family will agree."

She nodded but was reluctant to let go of his wrist. What was up with that? Was she clinging to him out of fear or was it something else?

She dropped her hand. "Still, I don't want to be a burden."

"Sounds like you're blaming yourself for this, but it's

not your fault, you know. Not at all. There's only one person to blame. If he's guilty of his actions, I aim to bring him to justice."

His rock-hard tone reminded her of Grady after he'd turned into a domineering guy, giving her a moment's pause. Grady had gone from sweet to tough in a flash like this, and she'd feared he would hit her. Thankfully, he hadn't, and he'd never called her names or otherwise verbally abused her.

"Sorry," Matt said. "I know that sounded harsh, but I can't handle when a man… Well, you know."

She nodded.

"Mommy, I need more syrup," Emilie said.

"Enjoy the pancakes." Matt gave her a lingering look and stepped from the room.

She poured the syrup, her mind racing. So many things to consider right now, and she didn't know what to focus on.

"I love you, Mommy," Emilie said out of the blue.

Perfect. Her daughter reminded her of the most important thing, and even with the loss of Troy, Nicole felt so blessed to be the mother of this precious child.

Nicole needed to banish all emotions and remember her every action had to be about keeping Emilie safe. That meant ignoring that she found Matt McKade attractive and evading Grady at all costs.

She would stay ahead of him. She had to. She couldn't fail, or the consequences would be dire not only for herself but for her baby girl, too.

"Have you checked out her story?" Matt's father asked from his recliner. His feet were planted firmly on the floor and his body rigid. Matt had expected both the posture and the question from his sheriff father, who questioned everything, at times trying Matt's patience.

Matt leaned against the wall, acting like it was no big deal, so his dad would relax, when this was a big deal for Matt. Huge deal. Especially after spending time with Emilie, raising thoughts of having a family of his own someday. He needed to be sure no one hurt her. Her mother, too, though she seemed a bit prickly about his help.

"I don't have all the details yet," he said to his dad and explained what he'd learned from dispatch. "But you should also know, this guy's an Austin police officer."

"Of all the..." Matt's granddad shot to his feet and ran a hand through hair still as thick now as when he'd been the Lake County sheriff. Many generations of McKades had filled that position, going back to the 1800s. "It's bad enough that this is happening to a woman, but by one of our own? That's not something I can abide."

"You're awful fast to believe her." Matt's father eyed his dad.

Matt's granddad planted his feet wide. "Don't give me that look."

"What look?"

"The one that says I've been out of law enforcement too long and don't know what I'm talking about." Matt's granddad crossed his arms. "I can read people as well as I used to, and there's something about that young lady that rings true."

"You only saw her for like a minute," Matt's father said.

He tightened his arms. "That's all it took."

Matt's father turned his attention to Matt. "What's your gut feel on this? Do you buy her story?"

"The background check I ran on her last night leaves me leaning toward believing her, but I don't know her well enough to be sure." Matt pushed off the wall. "Still, with a child in the picture, we need to err on the side of caution. I'd like her to stay here until the car's ready. Not only because Nicole doesn't have her wallet to pay for a motel, but also if a cop is stalking her, she won't fare very well on her own."

His mother sighed. "I don't like this. Not one bit. If this guy is after her, it doesn't seem very wise for her to take off before you look into this stalker. Especially when she can stay here with you all to look out for her."

"Problem is, Mom, she doesn't trust law enforcement. Means she doesn't trust me."

She gritted her teeth. "I wish I could tell her what a fine man you are. That you're an upstanding deputy and would give your life for her if needed."

Someone cleared their voice in the foyer, and he turned to find Nicole standing there, her assessing gaze fixed on him.

"Sorry to intrude." She held his gaze. "But I wondered if I might use your telephone to call my sister in Austin. I promised to check in with her by now, and she's likely worried. Thankfully, I'm a teacher and we're on Christmas break, so I don't need to call into work, too."

"You're welcome to use the phone," his mother said before Matt could get a word out to warn against it.

"I don't know if that's such a good idea," he said. "As a police officer, Harmon could track the call."

Nicole chewed on her lip for a moment. "Piper's at work by now, and she's employed by a huge company. Wouldn't the call just show as coming in on the main company line? Nothing direct to Piper."

"Depends on the system," Matt said. "It could also show a linked call to her extension. But still, I think the odds of Harmon getting access to the company phone logs is minimal. Just don't call her at home."

"Then thank you for the offer of the phone." The words came out on a sigh of relief, and Matt hated that she was having to go through this. "Maybe Piper can come up with an idea of how to get my wallet to me, too. I'd ask the bank to send a new card or have Piper send me the money, but that would take days, maybe weeks."

"Why doesn't Matt go get your wallet?" his grand-dad suggested.

"I was thinking the same thing," Matt said. It would also allow him to verify her story about the hunting knife and picture if Harmon hadn't gone back to remove it.

She arched a delicate eyebrow. "You wouldn't mind?"

He shook his head. "I'm off today and was just going to work on campaign stuff."

"That can wait," his father said. "The election is almost a year away, and a day off now shouldn't be a problem."

"Dad's the sheriff, and he's retiring," Matt told Nicole. "I'm running for his office. Granddad was the sheriff before him."

"Oh." Her tone was flat and didn't give away even a hint of what she thought about his statement.

He honestly hoped it would help sway her opinion of him, but he knew that she needed to see his actions not just hear his statements to earn her trust. "I'll head out after I arrange for your car to be towed."

She nodded. "You'll be careful, won't you? I mean, I'd hate for you to be hurt."

"I can tag along so someone has your back," his grand-dad said.

"Another good idea." Matt smiled at his grandfather, who would do just about anything to stay involved in law enforcement work. Matt didn't think there would be any trouble, but he'd love to have the company. "We'll take the farm truck instead of the squad car to keep from drawing attention to ourselves."

His granddad got a grin on his face. "But we'll be carrying."

Matt nodded. "That goes without saying."

"And you'll be careful that Grady doesn't follow you back here, right?" Nicole bit down on her lower lip.

"Now, little lady, don't you worry." Granddad puffed up his chest. "Matt's a fine deputy in a long line of fine deputies. He won't let this fella tail him. That you can be sure of. You need someone on your side, and the McKades are here for you. You can trust us."

Nicole nodded, but ongoing skepticism lingered in her expression. He hated seeing it. Not only as a deputy, and if he was honest, even more as a man who found himself interested in her. Not that he had time to court a woman or raise a family. He worked full-time as a deputy, often working overtime as it was, and then there was his campaign. He couldn't get distracted and lose the office his father and granddad had held for so many years and let them down.

So much pressure, but even if they had wanted this for him, he wanted the job for himself ever since he was a kid and looked up to his dad and granddad. He'd given up serious relationships to attain this goal, and once he was the best sheriff he could be, then he would look to his personal life.

So he needed to keep his mind on the job here. Only on the job. "If you'll give me your keys, I'll drop them at the garage before Granddad and I take off for Austin. Is there anything I can tell the mechanic about what happened before the car died?"

"Um, well…" She tilted her head, resembling Emilie when she'd peered up at him with her question about the horses.

"There was one thing," she said. "The headlights flickered a few times."

"Sounds like the alternator," his granddad said.

"If so, will that take long to repair?" she asked.

Granddad shook his head. "An hour or so if Clem has the part."

Matt expected that hearing she could leave town today would lighten Nicole's distress, but her eyes narrowed. "Where might I call my sister?"

Matt's mother stood. "Every bedroom has a phone, and I'm glad to keep an eye on Emilie while you make that call."

Nicole smiled. "She should be done eating by now, so that would be wonderful, thank you."

"Do you have other family in the area that you might need to call?" his mother asked.

Nicole shook her head. "Our parents live in Minnesota, and I don't want to worry them with this."

"Of course," his mother said.

They departed together, and Matt faced his father. "You'll be around to keep an eye out for Nicole while I'm gone?"

His father nodded. "But be careful, son."

Matt resented his father's warning. Matt was a good deputy and didn't need his father to tell him how to do his job. Matt had skills his father had never had at his age, but he'd never disrespect his dad by telling him that. "I'm always careful."

"I'm not talking about the job."

Oh?

His dad stood, planted his feet wide in the same stance most law enforcement officers used when confronting a problem, and Matt knew he wouldn't like what his dad had to say. "You're looking at the woman like a man on a desert island who hasn't seen a female in years. It could cloud your judgment."

"I'm not—"

"No point in denying it," his granddad interrupted. "Your dad is right. It's not hard to see. However, I don't happen to think that's a bad thing, because it's high time you started living life instead of living for your job. Seeing you interested in a woman for a change gives me hope."

Matt could hardly believe his granddad had said that when he had such high expectations of Matt as the next sheriff.

"A valid point." His father spun to peer at Granddad. "Just not one that applies to a woman in potential danger."

"Leave the boy be, Walt." Granddad crossed his arms. "He's got a good head on his shoulders, and you've trained him well."

Matt knew he needed to step in before this discussion turned into an argument. He changed his focus to his granddad. "Soon as I get everything settled with Nicole's car and run home to take a quick shower, I'll stop back for you, and we can make that road trip."

Excitement burned on his grandfather's face, and he clapped Matt on the back.

Matt gave him a smile of thanks and headed for the entryway. Nicole came down the steps, her keys jingling.

"My apartment key is on this ring, too." She handed the keys and a slip of paper to him. "I know you got my address last night, but I jotted it down for you."

He took the items, careful not to touch her hand. He hated to admit it, but his dad was right. She got to him, and he could only imagine what even one touch might do. "My family will be here while I'm gone. You need anything, you ask them, okay? They're on your side."

"Thank you." A tentative smile crossed her face.

He longed to solve her problem and put a wide smile like Emilie's there instead. And that was precisely why he stepped onto the porch to call Clem at the garage.

After he finished arranging to have Nicole's car picked up, he ran for his family's old truck. He fought against the brisk wind whipping from the north. This wind could signal a drop in temperature, not an unusual occurrence for December in the Texas Hill Country.

He took the truck to his apartment on the outskirts of Lost Creek, where he showered and changed into a comfy pair of jeans, his favorite boots, a button-down shirt and a heavy denim jacket. Back in the vehicle, he tuned in the local radio station to make sure there wasn't any snow forecasted for their area. With their elevation, it wasn't unusual to get a light dusting of snow at this time of year. The forecast came on just as he arrived at Clem's place on the other side of town. Snow flurries were possible, and the cold temperatures were forecast to continue for some time, but nothing to delay his trip.

He parked in a small area to the side of the ancient whitewashed building with a rusty metal awning. An old wrecker pulled into the lot hauling a white Honda Accord, the plates confirming it was Nicole's car. Matt hopped down and met Clem as he parked and got out of his truck. He was dressed in clean coveralls, the fabric straining over a large belly. His face sported heavy jowls and a roadmap of wrinkles from his many years in the Texas sun.

Matt handed over the keys. "The owner's phone is out of commission for the time being, so give me a call the minute you know anything, okay?"

"Sure thing," Clem said.

Matt shook hands with Clem before climbing back into the old pickup. His phone rang, and he checked the caller ID to see a call from Kendall. Hoping she'd gotten Austin PD to send the blotter records, he eagerly answered.

"I know you're off today," she said. "But you're gonna want to hear this. We had a shooting at the Wagon Wheel Motel. No injuries, but the guest staying in the room has cleared out. Was registered to an Otto Cutler."

Matt had never heard of the guy, but then that didn't surprise him, as a motel guest would most likely be from out of town. "You think it was an accidental discharge, and Cutler bailed to avoid being slapped with a misdemeanor?"

"Looks like more than that."

"Okay, so tell me."

"On a whim, I showed Grady Harmon's picture to Zeke." Zeke had owned and operated the motel for going on thirty years.

"And?" Matt asked, his interest piqued now.

"And he says Harmon was the guest registered as Cutler."

Matt's heart plummeted. "Harmon's here? In Lost Creek?"

"Looks like it, and that's not all. Tessa discovered something on a notepad in the room." Their other sister was Lake County's lead crime scene investigator. "Harmon removed the top page, but he'd left impressions on the page below. He'd written Nicole's name over and over like some crazed stalker."

Matt's gut tightened at the information. "And no sign of Harmon? His car, nothing?"

"Nothing."

"Let me know if you find anything else."

"You don't want to come over here?"

"Want to, yes. Going to, no. If Harmon's in town, he could know Nicole and Emilie are at the ranch. I need to make sure they're safe." Matt hung up and cranked the engine while calling his father's cell phone.

It went straight to voice mail. He had to be on another call.

Matt dialed the house.

One ring. Two. Three.

"C'mon. C'mon. C'mon."

The answering machine kicked in, which almost never happened. Someone usually answered.

Had Harmon gotten to them?

Matt could easily imagine the crazed stalker standing there, his gun on Matt's family, Nicole and Emilie.

The knot in Matt's gut tightened. He shifted into gear and spun out of the lot, praying as the tires rolled over asphalt that he would get to his family and the vulnerable pair before it was too late.

FOUR

"Can I sit on the horsey?" Emilie begged as she danced on her tiptoes. "Please, Mommy."

"I don't know." Nicole gripped Emilie's hand tighter and tried to take a step closer to the horse for her daughter's sake but couldn't move her feet.

"Beauty's a real sweetie." Winnie rubbed the white horse's neck poking over the corral rail, and Beauty seemed to love the attention. She didn't seem to mind that Matt's mother and his grandparents had brought Nicole and Emilie down to the corral to see her. Or mind that Emilie moved about impatiently, her arms gesturing wildly. Beauty simply stood there.

Nicole was the opposite. Her brain was screaming at her to bolt in the other direction and take her child with her. Nicole had been thrown from a horse when she was eight and it reared up. Her parents tried to get her to climb back on but she was just too afraid. Her fear lingered since then, and she consciously avoided them.

"Looks like you don't cotton to horses," Jed said.

"I don't."

"Nothing to be afraid of." Jed smiled, tightening the many laugh lines around his eyes. "Kendall's horse is as gentle as you are with Emilie."

"Still, I..." Nicole took a step back.

Betty rested her hand on Nicole's arm. "It sounds to me like you had a bad experience on a horse."

She nodded.

Winnie turned her attention on Nicole. "That can do it, but like Jed mentioned, Beauty's a sweetie, and Jed would never suggest putting Emilie on her back if he didn't think it was safe."

"I don't know." Nicole studied the horse's smooth coat and waited for her to rear up, just like the one that had thrown her.

The roar of an engine and sound of tires crunching over gravel as a vehicle raced up the driveway caught Nicole's attention. Terrified Grady had found them, her instincts kicked in, and she tucked Emilie behind her to turn to look. An old pickup truck barreled in their direction. Not Grady's, but he could be driving any vehicle.

Tendrils of fear wrapped themselves around her heart.

Betty squeezed her arm. "Don't worry. That's just Matt in the ranch truck."

"Does he usually drive like a maniac?" She wasn't surprised to hear the tremor in her own voice.

Concern appeared in Jed's eyes as he focused on his wife. "Take Nicole and Emilie into the house. The study's the safest place, and Walt's likely in there. I'll see what's going on with Matt."

Nicole wanted to know why Matt was racing to the door, but she had to think of Emilie over her own curiosity. She scooped her daughter into her arms and hurried toward the house right behind Betty, who traveled faster than Nicole could have imagined the older woman could move. On the steps, Nicole glanced back to see the truck still charging toward them.

Betty reached for the door handle, but Walt jerked it

open, his cell phone to his ear. "I heard the engine clear in my study. What's that boy up to?"

Before Betty or Nicole could respond, Walt pushed past them and jogged down the stairs. Betty stepped inside, and Nicole followed her down the hall to a room with a wide, wooden desk.

Betty gestured at a side chair. "Go ahead and have a seat while we wait."

Nicole shook her head. "I'm too antsy to sit."

"It's likely nothing." Betty smiled, but it was restrained and not at all convincing. She stationed herself at the door as if she was expecting a marauding army, raising Nicole's concern even more.

Emilie tugged on Nicole's hands. "Can I draw?"

"Walt keeps paper in the top left drawer," Betty said, but didn't turn to face them. "Help yourself."

Nicole didn't want to leave the doorway where she could see what was happening, but it was better to get Emilie away from the door. She carried her daughter to the other side of the desk and settled her on her lap. After retrieving paper and a pencil, Nicole placed them on the desk in front of Emilie.

"I want colors," she complained.

"A pencil will have to do for now." Nicole hugged Emilie, reveling in the feel of her child and reminding herself why they'd had to bolt from the corral. "Why don't you draw Beauty? She's white and the paper is white."

"I like Beauty." Emilie picked up the pencil and started drawing what Nicole assumed was the outline of a horse but looked more like an elephant.

Nicole tapped her foot, waiting for something to happen. The front door groaned open and footsteps came barreling down the hallway. An urgent conversation started with mumbled voices in the foyer, and her heart pounded so hard it was a wonder Emilie didn't feel it against her back and comment.

Betty stepped aside. Nicole instinctually tightened her arms around Emilie, but this had to be okay, right? Betty wouldn't stand down unless it was safe. At least, Nicole didn't think she would.

Matt burst into the room, his gaze searching like a heat-seeking missile and locking on Nicole. His face had lost his healthy tan, and gone was the composure she already associated with him.

She swallowed hard and waited for him to speak.

"Harmon's in town," he finally said.

"Are you sure?" Nicole's breath left her body, and she wasn't sure she could draw in another one.

"Pretty sure."

"Like how sure?"

Matt widened his stance, met her gaze and held firm. "Ninety-nine percent."

Thankfully, she was sitting down, or she would've fallen down. Her mind raced for a logical explanation for how Grady could be in Lost Creek but couldn't come up with one. "How could he have found us?"

Emilie swiveled to look at Nicole. "Who, Mommy?"

"An old friend." She was thankful Matt had called Grady by his last name so Emilie wouldn't have any idea who Matt was talking about.

Betty turned. "Emilie, my granddaughter Tessa just arrived with her dog, Echo. Would you like to meet Echo?"

Emilie's eyes widened, her eyes almost as wide as when she peered up at Beauty in what seemed like a lifetime ago. "Can I, Mommy?"

"Sure."

Emilie hopped down and ran across the room as

fast as her chubby legs could carry her. The sight usually brought a smile to Nicole's face, but right now she couldn't muster up even a hint of a smile. She concentrated on breathing and ridding her body of fear to think logically as Betty took Emilie's hand. Her daughter was in such a rush, she pulled Betty into the hallway.

"Slow down, sweetie," Nicole called out to her daughter to stop her from running Betty ragged.

Matt settled in a chair across the desk, his face still grim. "A gunshot was reported at a local motel. My sister Kendall responded to the scene. She's a deputy."

Still agitated, Nicole started fiddling with the corner of Emilie's drawing. Creasing. Unceasing the paper, but her concern still overwhelmed her, and she let it go to clasp her hands in her lap.

"All my siblings are in law enforcement," Matt said. "Tessa is a crime scene investigator. My brother, Gavin, is a Texas Ranger. And you know that my dad's the sheriff and Granddad once was, too."

"Runs in the family, then," she said, though honestly, right now she couldn't focus on his family history.

"For longer than you know." He lifted his powerful shoulders. "A McKade's been the county sheriff or a deputy for the last 125 years."

If she hadn't ever met Grady, she would have placed unequivocal trust in this man sitting across from her. Trusted his law enforcement family, too, but Grady had ruined that for her. Now she questioned her ability to assess other people's intentions and found herself doubting almost everyone.

With her and Emilie's lives at stake, Nicole had to be cautious and ask the right questions. "Is this gunshot somehow related to Grady?"

Matt nodded.

Nicole couldn't find the words to express the new terror racing through her body. She'd been feeling safe here. Perhaps already relying on the McKades too much. Maybe buying into the fact that they were as caring and compassionate as they seemed on the surface. But now, Grady was in town, and she couldn't do a thing about it. He didn't violate the restraining order just by being in town. If he'd tried to get close to her, then Matt could arrest him, but as it was, Grady was free to roam Lost Creek. She couldn't stay here any longer than it took to get her car repaired. She had to run again.

Matt was grinding his teeth and shifted his jaw before speaking. "Kendall showed his picture to the motel owner. He confirmed the room was registered to Grady under a false name. An Otto Cutler. Do you recognize it?"

She shook her head. "Wouldn't Grady need ID for Otto Cutler to register at the motel?"

"I haven't gotten the details from Kendall yet, but I know the motel manager is a stickler for his records. I suspect Grady had ID. Doesn't mean it was official. He'd know how to get a counterfeit one made."

Gunshots, counterfeit IDs and her, not things she ever thought would go together, and the thought ratcheted her fear up another level, heading toward panic. "How could I ever have made such a big mistake in dating him?"

Matt didn't answer right away as if he didn't want to fault her for this situation, a kindness she didn't expect from him. He watched her for a long moment, looking like he wanted to say something else, but then shifted his gaze over her shoulder. A good thing, as far as she was concerned. She thought after seeing several crosses on the walls that Matt was raised in a Christian household, and she was thinking of disclosing how she'd ignored

God, but Matt had no need to know what was going on in her life beyond the stalking.

His phone rang, and he answered while coming to his feet and shrugging out of a heavy denim jacket. She concentrated on watching him to keep her fear at bay. He'd changed into an emerald green long-sleeved shirt, and the color made his eyes look darker and even more dramatic. He'd also put on faded jeans that fit as if tailor-made for him and a pair of scuffed cowboy boots that looked like he'd worn them for years.

He listened intently but didn't say much other than yes and okay, and soon disconnected. "That was Clem at the garage. Like Granddad thought. Your car's alternator is bad."

Just the news she needed to hear. She could get on the road today. "An hour to fix it, then. If Grady *is* here, it means Piper can safely get my wallet and bring it to me, and we can leave the minute my car is finished."

"It's not quite that easy. Clem doesn't have the right part for your car. He'll order it and even spring for overnight delivery, but you'll still be spending the night here." Matt planted his hands on the desk. "And, with Harmon in town, I wouldn't want your sister coming here and putting herself in danger, too."

"Right. You're absolutely right." Nicole didn't want to stay the night, but how could she leave? She didn't have her wallet to rent a car or take a bus.

She'd just have to resign herself to spending one more night here. One night. She could do that.

Matt watched Emilie slip her hand into his mother's. She was taking the munchkin upstairs to read to her, allowing Matt and Nicole to talk to the recently arrived Kendall and Tessa. His mom and nana were deliriously happy to have a small child in the house, and he could easily imagine how spoiled the first of the next generation of McKades would be. Thankfully, that would be his brother, Gavin, and his wife, Lexie, or Tessa and her fiancé, Braden, once they were married, who had to worry about that, not him. Nor Kendall, as she was as single as he was. He wasn't planning on getting married anytime soon and without a wife he surely wasn't going to have a child.

Echo left Emilie and loped across the room to lay at Tessa's feet by the fireplace. The Labrador retriever dropped on her side, placing her shiny black belly to the fire. Previously in training to be a service dog for the deaf, she washed out and Tessa had adopted her. Echo stuck close to Tessa, even though his sister didn't need the dog's assistance.

"Bye, doggie," Emilie said as she turned the corner.

Nicole sighed. Was she sighing with worry or relief as his mother took Emilie out of the room?

Relief, probably. That's what Matt had felt when he'd arrived back at the ranch to find Nicole and Emilie sitting behind his father's big desk. He'd barely kept it together on the drive over. He'd always been levelheaded in the past, but in less than a day with these two, everything seemed to be changing far too quickly for his liking.

He glanced at Nicole. She had this cute button nose just like Emilie's, and her ice-blue eyes were the same, too. Maybe that was the reason for his unreasonable worry. Nicole reminded him of Emilie, and he had no doubt the little imp had already found a place in his heart. He could hardly believe he'd let them in so quickly. Could he be making a mistake by putting his work before considering a family of his own right now?

He remembered Emilie's excitement in seeing the

horses out the window. Her manners. The way she gazed up at him with such trust and innocence. The thoughts brought a smile to his face.

Yeah, worry for Emilie. That explained his crazy state of mind after learning about Harmon.

Kendall twisted her shoulder-length hair up into a clip, then leaned against the fireplace mantel. "What about this makes you smile?"

"Yeah, bro?" From the sofa, Tessa peered at him in much the same way she studied forensic evidence.

He hated that they were questioning him like this in front of Nicole, and he didn't bother to answer. "Who wants to bring me up to speed first?"

His sisters shared a knowing glance, and he frowned at them to discourage further comments.

Kendall's eyebrows went up. "Now you're cranky."

"I can't believe we'll be working for you soon," Tessa muttered.

He wanted to sigh, but he'd never seen his sheriff father or granddad sigh on the job, and he needed to start acting the way he believed he should behave when discussing work.

He looked at Nicole. "Normally, we wouldn't include a victim in our update meeting, but your safety is our top priority. To that end, we would question you about the details we plan to talk about and ask your opinion about Harmon so we can make the best plan to keep you safe, so it's best to have you involved now."

"I appreciate being included," Nicole said. "And if you need me to step out of the room at any time, I totally understand."

He nodded his understanding and turned his attention back to his sisters.

"A report, please," he said again, this time making sure he didn't sound cranky.

"I'll start," Kendall volunteered. "Zeke said Cutler checked in this morning. Didn't give an official departure date, but paid cash in advance for three days."

"Zeke's the motel owner," Matt told Nicole. "Did he ask for ID?"

Kendall nodded. "Harmon produced a Texas driver's license. Address was in Austin."

Just as Matt had suspected. "I suppose it's too much to hope Zeke made a copy of it."

"He didn't, but I ran a check on the name Otto Cutler with an Austin address. It returned a single record for a deceased male who died two years ago at the age of eighty."

"Not surprising," Matt said. "I figured you'd find something like that."

"Does this mean Grady took this dead man's identity?" Nicole curled her fingers into fists and rested her hands on her knees.

Matt shrugged. "He could've had a bogus driver's license made using the name, or he could have completely stolen the man's ID."

Nicole shook her head in wide sorrowful arcs. "The more I learn about him, the more I know I should never have dated him. I just can't believe I ever did."

"Hey." Kendall smiled. "Don't beat yourself up. We all make mistakes about people."

"I dated a guy who cheated on me." Tessa frowned and glanced at Kendall and Matt. "Turns out my family saw the signs, but me? Nah. I was blinded by love."

"I'm sorry about that." Nicole's gaze locked on Tessa's and it seemed like their mutual bad experiences with men cemented something between them.

Matt didn't know if he should say anything, but he was glad his sisters were able to offer some comfort along with their insights into the investigation.

"I'll keep looking into this," Kendall said, getting them back on track. "I ran the address and there's an Erma Cutler, seventy-six, still living at the residence. Likely his wife. I'll have Austin PD visit her to see what they can learn."

"Let me know if they discover anything that helps us." Matt smiled his thanks. "Zeke have anything else to say?"

She shook her head.

He turned to Nicole. "Before Tessa reports, you should know she located something in the motel room that might upset you."

"What?" Nicole crossed her arms as if trying to protect herself.

Matt didn't have the heart to tell her about the notepad. "Tessa, can you describe it?"

"I can do even better." She leaned down to her tote bag and took out a clear evidence bag holding the small hotel notepad. She handed it to Matt but kept her gaze on Nicole. "I located this notepad with impression evidence in his room. He wrote on the top sheet, but removed the paper, leaving impressions on the next page. If you hold the pad in the light, it's obvious that your name is written all over the page."

Matt looked up to see Nicole's face had blanched, and he hated to add to her concern, but he had to. "The indentations are deep. Means he must have written over the names several times. Like he's definitely gone past stalking to obsessing over you."

Nicole gasped.

"I'm sorry we had to bring this to your attention, Nicole," Tessa said. "But we thought you needed to know."

She nodded woodenly and held her hand out to Matt. "Can I see it?"

He handed over the bag. She moved closer to the sunlight streaming through the window and tilted the pad at an angle. She didn't speak but planted a hand on the wall as if she felt weak.

Kendall stepped across the room and took Nicole's arm. "C'mon. Let's sit."

The moment Nicole dropped onto the sofa, she handed the bag back to Tessa. "This confirms what I've been thinking. His texts were once pleading but their tone soon changed to threatening. And then the knife last night."

"Yeah, that seems to fit," Matt said.

Her eyes narrowed. "Can you use the notepad to find him?"

Matt shook his head. "I don't think it will help find Harmon, but if it turns out that he's charged with a crime, it can demonstrate his intense infatuation with you and perhaps help a jury to convict him."

Nicole frowned. "How would this help a jury when you can barely see it on the notepad? Seems to me they'd be skeptical."

"That's easy. I haven't processed it yet." Tessa's face took on the same rapt expression it held whenever she talked about forensics. "When I get back to the lab, I'll run it on an Electrostatic Detection Device. It will apply charges and toner to a film over the document and make the writing visible to the eye."

"You can do that?" Nicole asked.

"Tessa is the very best at forensics," Matt replied with no hesitation and maybe a bit of pride in his sister's many skills. "And you can be sure she'll use whatever she locates to help find Harmon or convict him."

"Thanks, Matt." Tessa sounded surprised.

Why the surprise, he didn't know. He praised her all the time, didn't he? Maybe not *all* the time. He would need to a better job of that if he became sheriff.

His father stepped into the room, and all eyes went to him. Matt only hoped if he was elected sheriff, he commanded the same respect he saw in his sisters' eyes. It was hard to think of being the boss of these women whose pigtails he'd pulled, and who he teased for most of their lives. Sure, he loved them and protected the two of them when they'd gotten older and had any problems, but still…their boss? That would be totally different for all of them. He respected their skills and abilities as officers, and he had to remember to see that first and let them do their jobs.

"Heard about the weapon discharge." His dad settled in his well-worn leather recliner but didn't lift his feet. "You thinking it's related to Harmon?"

Matt brought him up to speed on their findings. "Tessa was just telling us about the forensics."

His father focused on Tessa. "Did you recover the discharged slug?"

She nodded. "Located it in the wall above the bed. Looks like a 9mm to me, but I'll get it to ballistics as soon as I leave here."

A quick nod was often the only approval his dad gave, but occasionally he was more effusive, and that praise made up for the lack at other times. Gavin was the only sibling who hadn't been able to work for his father for long. He'd been so upset about a woman being shot on his watch and an ensuing disagreement with their dad that Gavin had taken off for several years. If Gavin had still been on the county force, he would be running for sheriff instead of Matt.

Matt had to admit he was glad things worked out this

way. He really didn't want to become a pencil pusher and budget master, but he did want his county to be run right, and he believed he was the right man on the force to make that happen. He'd do his very best, but only time would tell.

"Question is," his father said, "did Harmon discharge his weapon or did someone shoot at him?"

"No way of knowing that at this time," Tessa said.

"His duty weapon is likely a 9mm, but odds are long that he's carrying it." Matt turned to Nicole. "Do you happen to know the type of handgun he carries off duty?"

"No. I'm not comfortable with guns and didn't want to know anything about it." Nicole reached up and pushed a strand of wavy blond hair from her eyes.

Matt's hand rose involuntarily as if it had a mind of its own. He wanted to see if her hair was as soft as it looked.

He shoved his traitorous hand into his pocket.

He would *not* develop feelings for this woman. No way. He would head to his father's office, sit down at the desk and come up with a plan to keep her safe and find Harmon. That, and only that, was what he would do.

FIVE

The next morning after a breakfast of scrambled eggs, sausage and homemade biscuits, Nicole faced Matt in the foyer, where he was shrugging into his denim jacket. He thought he was going alone to her apartment, but she had different plans. He'd put off the trip to get her wallet until today because it had taken him longer than he'd expected to arrange for someone in the Austin Police Department to meet him at her apartment.

At first, she hadn't even wanted to involve them, as they would want her to file a report and that meant recounting the incident with the knife. She didn't expect they'd be able to prove anything, so why put herself through bringing up those details again?

But she'd given it some thought overnight, and if they had any hope of capturing Grady, she had to do everything she could to help. To that end, she planned to be there when Matt met the police.

She took a breath and prepared herself for his rejection. "I'm going with you to my apartment."

Matt shoved his hands into his pockets but didn't speak.

She cast a quick glance at Jed pulling on worn cowboy boots in the family room, but he didn't seem to have an opinion, nor did his wife, and Nicole figured her request wasn't all that farfetched.

She took a step closer to Matt, catching the scent of his minty soap. "Think about it, Matt. If Grady's in Lost Creek, it should be fine for me to go to Austin. And you said I had to file a report about the break-in with the Austin police. How can I do that long-distance?"

"By telephone," he said, his tone flat.

"It's better in person," Jed said, earning a frown from Matt. "'Sides, with Austin PD meeting us, Harmon would be nuts to try anything."

Matt curled his fingers into fists. "From how Nicole describes him, he might be nuts."

"I don't know about nuts, but he *is* off balance," Nicole admitted. "Still, he's here, and I'll be there."

"What about Emilie?" Matt asked. "There's no way I'm taking her to meet with the police and to look at a knife."

"Winnie and I'll be glad to watch her," Betty offered, and Nicole was thankful as she'd planned to ask them to do so. "We can bake some cookies. And Walt is still on vacation. He'll keep an eye on her safety."

Matt worked the muscles in his jaw and finally gave a firm nod but didn't seem the least bit happy about it. "We should leave right away."

Betty jumped to her feet. "Let me pack some drinks and snacks for you all."

"Now, Betty." Jed eyed his wife. "This is official police business, not a picnic."

She waved a hand at him. "It won't be long, and you'll be wanting a cup of coffee and some of my Christmas cookies."

Jed made a production of sighing, but there wasn't any real oomph behind it.

"I'll just say goodbye to Emilie." Nicole left the room before Matt could change his mind and went to the office where Winnie sat with Emilie on her lap. They were playing a matching game that looked well loved.

Winnie looked up. "Found this game in Walt's closet. He's a pack rat. You'd never know by looking at his office. Open the closet door and you might be taken out by an avalanche."

She chuckled, and Nicole laughed along. The more she learned about the McKade family, the more she was starting to believe they were good folk. Now, Matt, she still didn't know as he kept trying to hide his feelings while the others seemed to be open books.

Did he have a reason to hide them, or was he just like Grady and held his feelings close to the vest? Either way, she still couldn't find it in her heart to trust him.

Emilie hopped down and ran to Nicole. "Did you see the game, Mommy? I'm really good at it. She even said so."

"*She* is Mrs. McKade."

"Sorry." Her daughter cast an apologetic look at Winnie. "Mrs. McKade."

Winnie smiled. "Mrs. McKade is a mouthful. You can call me Winnie."

"Is that okay, Mommy?" She looked up at Nicole with a pleading expression.

Nicole nodded, though honestly, she preferred that her daughter continue to call adults by formal names, but now was not the time to get into it. She didn't want to give Matt time to find a reason to leave without her.

She scooped Emilie up for a hug. "I'm going with Matt on a little trip. Mrs. McKade wants you to help her bake cookies."

Emilie peered at Winnie. "You do?"

"No, sweetie, the other Mrs. McKade."

Her eyes scrunched. "There's another one?"

"Matt's grandmother. She's in the kitchen."

"Why don't I take you there?" Winnie offered.

Emilie squirmed to get down.

Nicole grabbed a quick hug before putting Emilie down and smiling at Matt's mother. "Thank you for all your help."

"You're very welcome," Winnie said. "I love children and can't wait until one of mine makes me a grandmother." She took Emilie's hand. "Sooner rather than later as far as I'm concerned."

Emilie towed Winnie from the room, and Nicole followed. After meeting three of the four McKade siblings she could easily imagine their children. Especially Matt's. They'd be dark haired with big brown eyes and heart-melting smiles. Not that he'd smiled much since she'd met him, but it had only taken a single smile from Matt for her to imagine how it might look if he reserved a special one only for her.

Wait. Was—was she thinking of how Matt would be as a father? She'd just met the guy. How could she be projecting that on him because of his care for Emilie?

She found him standing by a tall Christmas tree in the foyer with his granddad, who was nearly dancing to get out the door. Jed reminded her of Emilie in his enthusiasm. Nicole approached them. She'd passed this tree several times now and wanted to take time to look at the interesting ornaments, but with Matt's intense focus locked on her, now was not the time to do so.

"Ready to go?" he asked.

She nodded and grabbed her jacket from the coat hook.

"It'd be a tight squeeze for three in the pickup. We'll be taking Mom's car." He opened the door and stood back.

His grandfather slapped a worn cowboy hat on his head and raced out like a little boy.

"He's a bit eager. He misses his law enforcement days." Matt chuckled.

Nicole loved the lighthearted sound and grinned at him. She looked into his eyes and was surprised to find them glowing with joy. His gaze heated as it locked onto hers. Gone was the guarded intensity he'd been displaying, to be replaced by the interest of a man for a woman.

So, he found her attractive, too. That thought made her unreasonably happy, when she shouldn't care at all. He washed the look away as fast as it came, and now she wasn't even sure it had been there.

"Don't forget the snacks." Betty hurried into the foyer, carrying a basket lined with gingham fabric.

Matt took the basket. "Thanks, Nana."

She nodded and squeezed Nicole's arm. "If you get hungry, just ask. These two are likely to focus on their work and forget all about eating anything."

"Thank you," Nicole said.

"After you." Matt gestured out the door. "Just follow Granddad if you can catch up to him."

She headed down the steps into a blustery wind coming from the north. The cold weather and tree in the foyer made it easy to believe Christmas was only four days away, but everything else? The fear. Grady's presence in Lost Creek. All of that erased her Christmas spirit. Plus, she didn't know where she and Emilie would be on the big day. Wherever it was, Nicole would find a church service and try to make the day special for her daughter.

Jed stood by a silver SUV and held the back door for her. "I hope you don't mind sitting in the back. I think it's best for me to ride shotgun."

"Happy to." She slid in, and Matt set the basket on the seat next to her.

Once the doors were closed and the seat belts buckled, Matt punched her address into the GPS.

"I don't get the need for these electronic things to do our thinking for us," his granddad grumbled. "Kids don't even need to learn to read maps these days."

"I can turn it off if you want to navigate." Matt cranked the engine.

His granddad took off his hat and shook his head. "Might as well leave it now that you did all the work of entering the address."

Matt got the car on the road. For the first twenty miles or so, his eyes continuously went to the rearview mirror, looking for Grady, she supposed. But then the time between checks lengthened, and he seemed to relax a notch.

Jed turned to her. "Don't tell Betty, but I'd like some of that coffee right now, if you wouldn't mind grabbing one of the insulated mugs I know she packed."

Nicole smiled at him and reached for one of six tumblers nestled in the bag. She handed it to Jed and had to admit, she'd enjoyed how this generous family had so readily accepted her.

"Wouldn't mind a few cookies to go with it, either." He winked.

Nicole already loved this old guy. He was kind and serious and funny at the same time. She was beginning to think Matt took after him, except she didn't see Matt having as much fun. But then, he was focused on catching a criminal. She suspected when he wasn't focused on that, he might be fun to be around, too.

She passed a container of cookies to Jed, who turned to settle into his seat with a deep sigh of contentment.

Matt looked up in the mirror at her and rolled his

eyes good-naturedly. Nicole had to work hard to stifle a chuckle. His granddad started talking about recent law enforcement happenings in their community, and she listened in. She heard the compassion for victims in Matt's voice, and the outrage over people committing crimes in the community he clearly loved. And under it all, she also heard the love and passion for his job, something not common these days.

Jed twisted open his tumbler, and the heady scent of fresh coffee filled the car. He swiveled to look at her. "You have any idea how Harmon found you in Lost Creek?"

She shook her head and kept her gaze on the mirror, but he looked back at the road.

"You must have some thoughts on how Grady could have found us," she said.

"The usual ways, I guess." He trained his gaze on her again. "First, you can't be positive you weren't followed."

"That's true." She sighed as she just wanted Grady out of her life. Wanted to take Emilie home and have their life go back to normal.

"Is it possible that he planted a bug in a backpack or tote bag?" Matt asked.

She hated the idea, but after all that she'd learned about Grady of late, she had to at least consider it. "It's not likely but I suppose it's possible. I'll check when we get back."

"Even easier would be to attach a GPS tracker to your car."

"Not something that happened back in my day." Jed took a long sip of his coffee. "And I'm glad I didn't have to worry about such things."

"Let's stop by Clem's garage on the way home," Matt

suggested. "He can put the car up on a hoist, and we can look for a tracker."

"That would be good if you think it's a possibility."

"I do."

Just the thought of Grady placing a tracker on her car and knowing where she was at all times made her stomach roil, but it explained how he'd frequently showed up wherever she went.

Matt's phone rang, and he accepted the call via the display on his dashboard. "What's up, Tessa?"

"I finally got through all the fingerprints we lifted at the motel room and ran them through the database. As suspected, they matched Harmon's."

"But why would Grady's prints be in the database?" Nicole asked.

"All law enforcement officers are printed so we can eliminate their prints at crime scenes," Tessa said.

"Thanks, sis," Matt said and disconnected the call.

Worn out from stress of all these new discoveries, she leaned her head back against the seat. Soon the humming tires had her yawning. She hadn't slept much until the early hours of the morning, and she relaxed back for the rest of the drive.

"We're almost at your place," Matt said, and she opened her eyes to see him looking at her in the mirror. "And I need you to describe Grady's personal vehicle."

She stared out the window at the familiar scenery. "He drives a large Ford pickup. It's dark gray. I don't know the model or the year, but it's newer."

He nodded and turned onto her road. As their SUV approached the apartment complex, he slowed. Thoughts of her racing escape last night came flooding back, and Nicole's stomach tightened around her lunch. She'd acted all brave when she'd told Matt she was coming along today, but right now she felt like one of the big chickens she'd seen at the McKade ranch.

He drove past the turn-in.

"That was my parking lot," she said.

"We're surveilling the place first," Jed replied, that excitement she'd heard earlier burning in his voice. "We'll drive by, and if it all looks good, we'll turn around."

She watched out the window for Grady's pickup. With most people who lived in these apartments at work, the lot was nearly empty, and it was easy to determine that Grady's truck wasn't there.

"Austin PD's not here yet," Jed said.

Nicole didn't like that, but what could she do? Ask Matt to drive on and come back later? Now that they were there, they might as well go inside.

"I don't see a problem with that, do you?" Matt asked his granddad.

"Nah. We're both carrying and can take care of Nicole." The confidence in his voice helped ease Nicole's concern a smidgen. "With this not being your jurisdiction, can you even act if you see Grady?"

"Law enforcement officers can act in any jurisdiction in exigent circumstances, like needing to protect a life." Matt turned around in the last parking lot. "Which building?"

"Third one on the right."

He swung the SUV into the lot and parked. She took a long breath and reached for her handle, but by the time she got the door open, Matt was standing there.

"To keep from contaminating the scene." He handed her latex gloves and booties to cover her shoes, then donned the same protective gear. "Stay between me and Granddad and no dawdling. Straight up the walkway."

He needn't have worried. She wasn't about to hang

outside and risk her life. She got out and moved closer to him than he'd probably like. His granddad, with his hand on his sidearm, joined them. They hurried through the frosty wind to her door. Matt stood back as if waiting for her.

"You have my keys," she said.

"Oh, right." He dug them from his coat pocket and handed them to her.

She opened the door, and the warm smell of cinnamon-scented pinecones she'd put in the fireplace greeted her, giving her a bit of comfort. She flipped on the overhead light, and her gaze went straight to the knife on the counter. "It's still there."

"Wait here with Granddad." Matt closed the door behind them. "I want to make sure no one is here."

"In the apartment?" She couldn't control her mounting fear, and her voice squeaked.

"Just a precaution," Matt said, but still, he drew his gun and made his way into the living area. He moved with confidence and stealth.

If she wasn't worried right now, she'd be impressed with him, but all she could think about was last night, when she'd been so very alone here and terrified that Grady was in Emilie's room. She cast a glance at the knife. It lay there, big and bold, and she backed away.

"Don't worry, little lady," Jed said. "Matt's the best deputy there is. Not just in our county, and I'm not saying that because he's my grandson. He takes his job seriously. Lives for it in fact and trains all the time. You couldn't have a better law enforcement officer at your side."

Nicole nodded. She was thankful for Matt's help—for his skills—but she couldn't help comparing him to Grady again. He lived for his job, too. Trained. Worked all the time.

Those things might make a great law enforcement officer, but a good man they did not necessarily make.

So why on earth couldn't she seem to contain this attraction to him? She had to get a grip on it before she foolishly let another man who was wrong for her into her heart.

SIX

After Austin PD Detective Frank Dawson arrived at Nicole's apartment and settled at the minuscule dining table, Matt picked up the knife from Nicole's kitchen counter to inspect it. He'd half expected Harmon to come back and take it to eliminate the evidence, but she hadn't reported the crime and maybe he figured it wasn't worth the risk of being seen entering her apartment.

Matt studied the knife. Nicole was right. It looked like a hunting knife, and he thought there was a trace amount of blood near the hilt. Likely from hunting, but he could be wrong. At least it hadn't been used on Nicole.

He looked at her sitting at a table in the dining area with the detective. Matt's granddad sat with them to protect her from a pushy detective, his granddad had said, gaining a tight smile from Nicole.

But now she'd wrapped her arms around her waist and kept darting a look at the knife as if she expected it to take flight and stab her. Matt wished he'd had the foresight to be the one to sit with her instead of checking out the knife. Not that he didn't trust his granddad to have her back, but Matt wanted to be there by her side.

A knock sounded on the door, and she lurched to her feet.

"Relax." Frank stood. "That'll be my forensic tech."

He went to answer the door, and Matt laid the knife on the counter. He stepped over to Nicole. "You said Harmon was a hunter, right?"

She nodded but her gaze remained fixed on the door, where a squat woman wearing an overly large Tyvek suit, bunched above a belt, entered the apartment. She wore booties over her shoes and dangly Christmas earrings with tiny twinkling lights. She was holding several cases, and her gaze wandered the space. When it landed on Matt, Nicole and Granddad, the tech frowned. She likely figured they'd contaminated the scene, but Matt had taken great care to protect the scene and made sure that no one but him had touched anything.

"Veronica is the best tech on the team," Frank said, "and rarely handles such simple investigations. We're grateful to have her."

"Simple?" Nicole cried out.

Granddad stood and puffed out his chest. "Nothing simple about a man threatening a sweet lady like Nicole."

Veronica cocked a thick eyebrow. "And you are?"

"Jed McKade," he snapped out in a tone he usually reserved for lawbreakers. "Former Lake County Sheriff."

"And I'm Lake County Deputy Matt McKade." Matt made sure his tone was softer to erase the woman's tight look. "This incident came up on our local radar."

Veronica deepened her frown. "You all must be well connected to get me assigned to this puny case."

Matt didn't acknowledge his connections, nor did he mention Harmon. He hoped Frank would keep his mouth shut, too, as he worked with Harmon and Matt didn't want word to get back to Harmon that Nicole had filed a complaint and that the Austin police department had processed her apartment. If they located any incriminating evidence, Harmon might become even more committed to finding Nicole.

"Let me show you where the knife was found." Matt stepped over to the counter without waiting for Veronica to agree. She followed him and set her cases on the kitchen floor.

"My sister is a crime scene investigator. I know how hard you work and how important your job is," he said in hopes of improving her attitude.

"I don't need someone telling me how great I am while I work," she grumbled. "I already know I'm great."

Okay, then. "The knife was stabbed in the photograph. Nicole removed it. Means you'll find her prints on it."

"Anyone else touch it?"

"I picked it up, but while wearing gloves. And unless someone broke in here since she left last night, no one has touched it."

Veronica snapped on a pair of gloves and then bagged the weapon.

"Looks like blood near the hilt," he said.

"I've got eyes," she said.

Matt never thought he'd crave having his sister on a case as much as he did now.

At the table, he met Frank's gaze. "You sure this knife will be thoroughly processed?"

Frank nodded. "Veronica's the best."

"I heard that," she said. "Don't appreciate being talked about."

"Not even when I brag on you?" Frank joked.

She snorted.

Talking to or about Veronica was getting them nowhere, and Matt wanted to finish up here and get on the road before dark. "Where do we stand with the report?"

Frank opened the case for his tablet computer, perched

his fingers over the keyboard and peered at Nicole. "Time to tell me what happened. Start at the beginning and don't leave anything out."

"Except the suspect's name," Matt said. CSIs liked to compare investigations, and he didn't want their conversations to get back to Harmon.

"Right," Frank said. "Just refer to him as the suspect."

Nicole glanced at Matt, looking like she needed reassurance. He smiled at her. "We're here with you and nothing bad can happen. Just tell Frank what you told me last night."

Silence stretched out between them like she was warring with what to do. He pressed his hand over hers resting on the table. "Go ahead."

She could easily pull away, but she didn't move her hand, making him unreasonably happy. He wasn't happy that she felt like she was in danger, but he could totally understand how she felt and wanted to help. Just the thought of her discovering the knife with sweet, little Emilie asleep in the other room made his gut hurt. He couldn't wait to get his hands on Harmon and snap on the cuffs.

"I came home from work," Nicole started and was soon sharing details of the night just as she'd reported them to him.

Matt glanced at his granddad, who gave a pointed look at Matt's hand still covering Nicole's. He frowned at his granddad's verbal message telling Matt it wasn't a good idea to get personally involved with a victim, but Matt no longer thought of Nicole that way.

Okay, fine, she was a victim, but she was so much more than that. She was Emilie's mother. A woman. A beautiful woman. Vulnerable, too. And a woman who made his heart beat faster, even when he knew it wasn't a good idea to get involved with her when he had to focus on the upcoming election.

He should follow Granddad's direction and remove his hand, but if he did, he might interrupt her story when she was recalling the events at a speed that kept Frank's fingers flying over the keyboard. He occasionally paused to ask a follow-up question, but for the most part, he let her talk like a good detective would. When she finished, she pulled her hand free and sat back in her chair, looking exhausted.

Frank stopped typing and looked up. "I'll just need your driver's license to finish the official report, and then you'll be good to go."

"I'll grab it for you." Matt had seen her wallet on the entryway table and went to retrieve it, earning an irritated glance from Veronica, who was dusting for fingerprints nearby.

Matt handed the wallet to Nicole, and she gave Frank her driver's license.

He entered the information and swiveled his tablet. "I need you to review this to be sure it's all correct. If it is, go ahead and sign on the screen with your finger."

Matt didn't know what to make of Frank requiring a signature. Many departments didn't require one from the person filing an incident report. But if a detective didn't believe the person's story, he might insist on a signature. Matt wasn't sure if that was the case here, but he would follow up with his Austin PD contact to confirm the report was filed and the evidence logged and processed.

Oblivious to Matt's inner turmoil, Nicole read the report and signed.

Frank took the tablet back, looked at it for a few moments, then gave a clipped nod. "That's it, then. If you leave a key for Veronica, she'll lock up, and you're free to go."

Nicole ran to a kitchen drawer to grab a key faster than he thought possible. She was clearly eager to leave her apartment. Not surprising. Matt wondered if she would ever be able to live here again.

Matt stood and focused on his granddad. "Will you take a look outside?"

"Roger that." He hurried outside.

To lighten her mood, Matt smiled at Nicole as they walked to the door. "Same instructions for the trip to the car."

She stopped by the doorway and rested a hand on his arm. She looked up at him, her gaze filled with gratitude. "Thank you."

He tried not to react to her touch, but the warmth of her hand traveled to his heart, making him very aware of her as a woman, and all he could do was stare at her. Her eyes creased, and she looked awkward and uncomfortable before she jerked her hand away.

Nice one, McKade. He'd made her feel bad for touching him. Not what he wanted to do at all. He smiled again. "Thank you for what?"

"For being here for me. I couldn't have told that story again without your support."

"I was honestly worried you might be offended by my actions."

"Why?"

He lowered his voice. "There seems to be this intense thing going on between us. I think you've noticed it, too."

"I have." She paused for a long moment. "It would be hard to miss."

"I wanted you to feel supported, but I didn't want you to think I was coming on to you."

"I didn't."

"Good. Good. I'm not available right now and don't want to lead you on."

Her eyebrows lifted. "You're in a relationship?"

"Yeah, with my job." He chuckled. "Seriously, with the upcoming election, I have to give my all to the job right now."

"I understand," she said. "We're on the same page here. After my relationship with Grady, it'll take a long time before I can trust a man again. Besides, we live in separate towns, and I have Emilie to focus on right now."

"Understandable," Matt said, but he hated that she just as good as admitted she still didn't trust him. He didn't like that in the least.

Was he starting to think about a relationship with her? He could imagine life with the two of them. Coming home from a tough day at work. Finding her and Emilie's smiling faces waiting to greet him.

Right. That was exactly what he shouldn't be thinking about.

Regardless, he would make sure she knew she could trust him. That he would change, no matter what it took.

A bitter wind skittered across the apartment parking lot, and Nicole shivered. She wasn't sure if it was because the sun had disappeared behind the horizon thus dropping the temperatures or because she feared Grady was hiding in every shadow around the property. Or nearly as scary, that she was letting herself get close to Matt, despite knowing better.

Matt opened the SUV's back door, and she slid into the warm car. When his granddad had returned from checking out the area, Matt had gone out to turn on the heater to warm up the vehicle. Now it was toasty and so was her heart from his thoughtfulness. Grady would never have done such a thing.

Stop. Just stop comparing Matt to Grady.

Sure, they were both law enforcement officers, but she was starting to see that was where the similarities ended. If she kept focusing on that, she'd forget her intentions to keep things professional between her and Matt, and that would do neither one of them any good.

Jed grabbed a tumbler of coffee from the basket and handed it to her. He passed another over the seat to Matt and took one with him to the passenger seat. On the drive home, they sipped on the warm drinks and conversation was at a minimum. She savored each sip of the rich coffee and thought ahead to the trip to Clem's garage. She was as wrung out as an old dishrag after recounting the attack again, and she didn't know how she might react if it turned out that Grady had tracked her car.

She closed the empty tumbler and put it in the basket. "Do you really think we'll find a GPS device on my car?"

Matt glanced in the rearview mirror. "Wouldn't be far-fetched for a police officer to plant one. He's likely up on all the latest surveillance techniques."

"I suppose."

"I been thinking," Jed said. "What if he found you another way?"

Matt glanced at his granddad. "How?"

"Kendall requested the blotter information from the Austin PD, right?" Jed swiveled and alternated his gaze between Matt and Nicole. "What if the officer she talked to is a buddy of Harmon's? He coulda told him about the request and mentioned that it came from Matt's office."

"I was hoping the department was big enough that it wouldn't happen, but it's a possibility," Matt said.

Nicole much preferred this explanation to a tracker

on her car. She was holding out hope that Grady wasn't *that* sneaky and that the visit to the garage would prove her right. She wanted to put it off, but it seemed like only moments later that Jed was pulling out his phone to call Clem. It was nearly seven, and the garage had closed at six. Jed had to convince Clem to come out on the cold dark night to meet them. But, of course, he got Clem to agree.

Nicole could easily imagine Jed as the sheriff, getting others to do his bidding with his persuasive charm.

Jed's stomach rumbled, and he leaned between the seats to grin at Nicole. "I best have a few of those cookies, or I might die of hunger before we get home."

Nicole tried to smile at him as she passed the container forward, but her stomach remained tied up in knots, and she didn't manage it. Keeping his gaze on her, he opened the container and offered the colorful frosted sugar cookies to her. She shook her head.

"You don't know what you're missing." He lifted the largest one out of the container. "My Betty's the best baker in the county. Maybe even in Texas."

Nicole enjoyed seeing how much he was still in love with his wife after so many years of marriage. Nicole had once thought she and Troy would have the same thing, but that wasn't to be. Would Matt find that with someone someday?

A pang of jealousy nipped at her. She had no right to be jealous and God warned about that very thing but it was there, telling her again how careful she needed to be not to fall for him.

Matt grabbed a cookie, and before long he and his granddad had polished off most of them, and they were pulling up to a ratty-looking garage. The bright interior light beamed through the window into the darkness, alleviating a bit of Nicole's apprehension.

Matt parked close to the front entrance and was out beside her door in a flash. He stood strong and ran his gaze over the area before opening the door. She waited for him to warn her to hurry inside, but he simply stepped back.

She didn't need a warning and hopped out. Matt directed her to a connecting door to the garage stall where a man wearing greasy coveralls held a remote control in his hand.

He glanced over his shoulder, revealing a dark smudge on his cheek. "Just putting the car up on the hoist now."

Matt introduced her to Clem, then grabbed a work light on a long cord from a nearby bench. The hoist stopped rising, and Matt stepped up to the rear bumper of her car. Nicole still hoped they wouldn't find a tracking device, but now that they were in the garage, she had a burning desire to know for sure. She joined Matt while Clem and Jed stood nearby, chatting about community happenings.

Matt ran the light over the underside of the bumper. He inspected it thoroughly before moving on to the front fender.

"Why are you looking in these particular spots?" she asked.

"GPS devices depend on signals from satellites above. Means they won't work if placed under something thick, like the actual body of the vehicle."

"See anything?" she asked.

"Not yet." He pivoted and moved to the nearest wheel well.

She tailed him. He slowly ran the light over the area, then quickly moved on to the next wheel well, where he stood staring.

"What?" She eased closer, her heart starting to beat faster.

He pointed at something that looked like a small black box. "It's a tracker."

Nicole reached up to touch the box, emotions crashing over her.

"Don't touch it," Matt warned. "I'll get Tessa out here to process it for fingerprints."

Nicole stared ahead. She could hardly believe what she was looking at. It was such an invasion of privacy from a man who had already violated her in so many ways. She started shaking, and no matter how hard she tried to stop it, she couldn't.

"Hey, hey." Matt took her hand, the warmth doing nothing to stop her anxiety. "Harmon may have put this here, but it ends now. This and any other chance he has to get close to you or Emilie. You have my word on that."

His care and compassion choked her up, and she had to swallow hard to stop tears of gratitude from flowing. She wanted to give him a hug to show her appreciation.

Stop. Now. Get a grip. Keep this professional.

Wise words, but unfortunately, she was finding it hard to follow her own advice.

SEVEN

Matt didn't like the way Nicole's face had paled, and every time he'd glanced in his rearview mirror on the way to Trails End, his family ranch, proved she hadn't gotten her color back. Not even when they stepped inside and Emilie ran to greet them. The little cutie was fresh from a bath, her curls damp, and she wore fuzzy blue footie pajamas with big white snowflakes.

"Emilie's had her dinner," his mother said. "But the rest of us waited for you all to eat."

Matt couldn't believe how blessed he was to have such wonderful parents. Always there for him. Supporting and caring for him. He wished Nicole had the same thing in her life here in Texas. That Emilie had an extended family like his parents, who provided for him. No child could go wrong under their guidance.

He circled his arm around his mother's shoulders and gave her a hug. "Thanks, Mom."

"Yes, thank you," Nicole said. "I'll just put Emilie to bed."

Emilie scooted out of her mother's reach. "Want Matt to do it."

Nicole shook her head. "I'm sure he wants nothing more than to eat his dinner."

"Please." Emilie turned her big blue eyes on him.

He might not have eaten for a year, and he would still be powerless to say no to those eyes beaming up at him. "I'd be glad to take you up."

She charged at him and hugged his leg. "And read a story?"

"And read a story." He swung her up into his arms and loved the clean scent of her shampoo, and he could imagine her bath time giggles.

How had he gone from not thinking about kids to thinking about a child's fun in the bathtub?

"Night, Mommy." Emilie gave a little wave to Nicole, who was frowning.

"Good night, sweetie."

Emilie settled her head against his chest with a sigh, and Matt started up the stairs. "Did you have a fun day with my nana?"

"I like her. She made me a dough ornament. One for Mommy, too, but don't tell her. It's a spuprise."

"A spuprise?" Matt asked confused.

"You know. She doesn't know about it."

"You mean surprise."

"That's what I said."

Matt nodded. "Wouldn't dream of telling your mom."

"I like dreams."

Matt pushed open the door to the room she was sharing with Nicole.

"I have my own bed now. It's because Nana said I'm a big girl."

He wasn't surprised to see his mother or Nana had added a small rollaway bed for Emilie and dressed it with warm flannel sheets, covered in snowflakes, much like the ones on Emilie's pajamas.

He didn't comment on the fact that she called his

grandmother Nana as if she were her very own grand-mother. His nana had likely insisted. He felt an odd amount of satisfaction in that. Too much.

He settled her into the bed.

She scooted into a sitting position and drew her knees up to her chest. "Don't forget my story. Books are in my backpack."

He dug into the pink bag covered in brown monkeys and pulled out three books. "Which one do you want?"

"The Night Before Christmas."

He sat on the bed, and she climbed up into his lap, her fuzzy pajamas catching on his scruffy chin. She wiggled into place as she had at breakfast, and his heart filled with the joy of holding such a special, trusting little girl.

She flipped the book open to page one, and he started reading. Before long, her head started drooping, and by the time he'd reached the final page, her head was resting on his arm, the soft curls tickling his skin. He closed the book and eased her around without waking her to settle her under the covers. He tucked them up tight to her chin.

He sighed and turned to leave. His mouth fell open.

"Sorry," Nicole said from where she stood in the door-way, holding a well-loved Mr. Monkey. "I just came up to tell you she won't sleep without this guy but looks like you have the touch."

His heart swelled at her comment. "I think it has more to do with her busy day with my mom and nana."

She smiled. "They said they had fun, too."

Matt looked back at Emilie, her soft hair curled around her chubby face, her thumb in her mouth. "How could you not have fun with her?"

"Grady didn't much like having her around."

Matt spun. "Then he's a fool."

His words came out more forcefully than needed, and

Nicole jerked back as if he'd slapped her. He'd been too sharp with her. "I'm sorry. I wasn't mad at you. Just at the guy who could hurt you and Emilie."

She nodded, but it wasn't hard to see she still was leery of him. Made him even madder but he tamped it down and forced out a smile. "We should get down to dinner. I know they'll be waiting for us."

Nicole nodded. "Let me just tuck Mr. Monkey in, and I'll be down."

She brushed past him, and he should have moved to leave but he couldn't. He was riveted in place. He watched her bend over her daughter, strands of Nicole's blond hair mixing with Emilie's. His heart sang at the sight. He could only be feeling a fraction of what a parent might feel, but even that was enough to fill him with longing for something he just couldn't have in his life right now.

Nicole placed a kiss on her daughter's forehead and slowly stood. She met his gaze and held it for a long time. Electricity charged between them. It was so intense that he was sure the crackle sounded in the air. She broke the hold and started for the door. He lingered for a moment to blow out a breath and flipped on the nightlight before silently closing the door behind him.

"You're good with her," Nicole said as she headed for the stairs. "Do you have nieces or nephews?"

He shook his head. "Gavin's the only one who's married, but I doubt it'll be long before he and Lexie start a family. Tessa's engaged, too."

"But you like kids?"

"Yeah, I mean I guess so. I haven't been around a lot of them, but if Emilie is any indication, I like kids." He chuckled.

She turned at the top of the stairs and held his gaze for the longest moment. "You likely got it from your parents and grandparents. They seem to be incredible role models."

"I was just thinking the same thing about them," he said. "I know how blessed I am to have been raised by them. What about your family?"

"They're great, but I think I mentioned that they live in Minnesota. My husband's job brought us to Austin. When he died I thought about moving back to Minnesota, but I discovered I didn't want to leave Austin."

"And your sister?"

"I was pregnant when Troy died, and Piper came down to help me. She ended up staying, too. Neither of us could face all the snow and cold again."

"What's a body got to do to get you two to come down so we can eat?" his granddad asked from the bottom of the stairs.

The corners of Nicole's mouth tipped in a big smile. "I just love your grandfather."

Matt sucked in a breath. She was stunning. Literally stunning when her eyes and face lit up with such happiness. He wanted to see that look, and only that look, on her face for the rest of her life. Not that he'd be with her, but he sure wanted to be the one to make her smile like that, not his granddad.

She turned and jogged down the stairs.

Matt took his time, letting all his warring emotions settle down before he had to sit in the dining room next to this woman who he couldn't remain neutral about despite his desire to keep her at arm's length.

From the plaid family room sofa, Nicole ran her gaze around the room. Walt sat in a big leather recliner, Jed in an overstuffed armchair, and Betty and Winnie next to her on the sofa. Matt leaned against the wall by a roaring fire, the flames flickering in the room lit only by a single lamp. Colorful stockings hung on the mantel holding an antique clock, and lights from the Christmas tree twinkled in the foyer. She felt like she was in a Norman Rockwell painting from times gone by, and she liked it. Loved it actually. She felt so secure. Safe. Protected. And cared for.

The entire McKade family had all come to her rescue, and she would hate walking out that door tomorrow, but walk out she would, even if she liked every McKade she'd met thus far. Even Matt, as much as she didn't want to admit it. She'd hardly been able to pull her eyes away from him and Emilie when he'd carried her up the steps. Her daughter had looked so small and content in his strong arms. He was proving to be such an amazing man.

What would it be like to be held by him? Resting her head against his chest. Comforting and exhilarating at the same time, Nicole suspected.

"Perhaps if you told us more about your relationship with Harmon, you might reveal information that might help us locate him," Walt said.

Poof. Her good mood vanished, and she readjusted her thinking. "What do you want to know?"

"How did you meet?" Winnie asked.

"I'm a teacher, and he came to talk to my class about safety." The memory was a good one, and a smile came to her mouth. "He was so good with my kids, and I think that hooked me right off the bat."

"But he didn't like having Emilie around, right?" Matt asked, reminding her of their conversation upstairs and making her think.

Was she letting Matt's affection for Emilie suck her in, like Grady had first done with her students?

She would have to be careful of that. "Right. He was

good that day in the classroom but turns out he wasn't a fan of having a child around all the time. Not that he ever hurt Emilie, or even got irritated with her. He just kept trying to find ways to pawn her off on Piper so we could be alone."

Matt eyed her, and that anger that had darkened his eyes upstairs when she talked about Grady was back. It was looking more and more like he had a temper. Maybe she was too hasty to think he and Grady didn't have a lot in common.

"What happened after that first meeting?" Jed asked.

"Grady pursued me with intensity, and we started dating right away. It was smooth sailing until he found out that Troy's job in advertising had paid very well, and I'd once led a privileged life that Grady couldn't give me."

"Is Troy Emilie's father?" Betty asked.

Nicole nodded. "He died when I was pregnant with her."

"So Harmon was put out by not making as much money as your late husband," Matt said.

"Yeah, he didn't think he could provide all the things that Troy had given me, and he started to feel insecure. I told him I didn't care about money and things. Honestly, I like a simpler life than I led with Troy, but Grady didn't believe me."

Walt shifted in his recliner. "What did he do about it?"

"He already worked a second job as a security guard, and he increased his hours." She shook her head. "The last month we dated, it really started to intrude on our time together. And his attitude. He'd get phone calls all the time, take one look at his caller ID and get mad."

"Who was calling him?" Matt asked.

"I'm not sure. He'd leave the room to talk and said he

couldn't tell me about the calls because they were work related."

Matt pushed off the wall. "If only we could get a look at Harmon's phone records. Maybe we'd find something to help us nab him."

She was confused. "I thought law enforcement looked at phone records all the time."

"Yeah," Walt said. "But only when we have probable cause for a warrant. In this case, we don't."

"There's got to be something you can do."

"Best we can do is request historical location tracking information," Matt said. "The state of Texas allows us to get these records without a warrant, but they're six months old."

"And that will help, how?"

His forehead furrowed. "I don't know until I see them, but these frequent calls could have started before you met him, and his other job might give us a bead on his location."

Walt nodded. "If the logs don't reveal his secondary employer, we should also contact all security firms in the Austin area to see if he works for any of them."

"He might not have contracted through a security firm and worked directly with a given company," Matt said. "Getting that information will be far more difficult."

"What about Harmon's family and friends?" Jed asked.

Nicole didn't have to think about that for long. "He doesn't have any close friends that I know about, but his parents and a brother live in Austin."

"Do you know where?" Matt asked.

She shook her head. "He wasn't close to them and never wanted me to meet them."

Matt arched a brow as if that meant something to him.

Maybe it did. She'd read how abusive men tried to isolate the women they wanted to control. Sure, Grady hadn't physically abused her, but he had wanted to control her life.

"I don't want to alert his family in case they are in touch with him, but I'll check into finding and questioning them if we run out of leads to work," Matt added. "What about social media? Did he have a Facebook or other social media account?"

"Grady? No. As a police officer, he didn't want his private information on the internet. He even hated that I used it. Said I was just asking to be scammed." Or maybe now in hindsight it was more that he wasn't in control of the people she communicated with on social media.

Matt frowned. "I hate to agree with Harmon on anything, but you have to be careful online. I'll do an internet search to see if it brings up any information on him."

"Has Tessa found anything on the tracker?" Jed asked.

"No prints and it's such a common model there's no way to track down the purchase," Matt replied.

Betty yawned. "Sorry, Nicole. I'm interested in your story, but your little sweetheart plum wore me out today, and I think I'll turn in."

"I'm with you." Jed stood and helped Betty to her feet.

Arm in arm, the older couple left the room, and Nicole's heart melted over their ongoing sweetness. "How long have they been married?"

"Fifty-eight years," Walt said.

"I only hope we can be as fortunate." Winnie smiled at her husband.

Nicole glanced at Matt, whose fond expression lingered on his mother. It was hard to believe he was so opposed to a relationship when he had such wonderful role models. But then, she was opposed to it right now, too, and her parents and grandparents were happily married as well.

"We should head up, too." Winnie gave Walt a pointed look before turning to Nicole. "Please tell me you've decided not to leave tomorrow."

"Sorry," Nicole said and was surprised to discover she actually meant it. "With Grady in town, I'm even more convinced it's best for us to go."

Winnie looked at Nicole, her expression open and warm. "I still think it's best for you to stay with us, but I won't try to convince you. Just know if you run into any trouble you can always call. And know that we are praying for you both."

Nicole was so touched by this woman's kindness that she gave her a hug. She'd grown attached to this God-fearing family in record time, and her failure to consult and listen to God made her feel undeserving of their care. What would they think of her if she told them about her struggle? Would Winnie still be hugging her?

"You can trust Matt," she whispered. "He may be my son, but there is no finer gentleman out there. He always keeps his word, and he's a top-notch deputy to boot."

Nicole remembered similar words from Jed, though he'd only mentioned Matt's work when Winnie meant the whole man. It would be so easy to give in right now in the embrace of the woman's arms and stay with them at the ranch. To trust Winnie's judgment of her son. Even more important for Nicole, to actually believe she could trust her own judgment in men again. But she simply wasn't ready for that.

She pulled back.

Walt crossed the room and offered his hand to Winnie. "My wife's right as usual. I hope you'll reconsider and stay."

Winnie faced Matt. "I made up the bed in your old room."

"Guess you figured I'd be staying the night."

"I knew you wouldn't leave Nicole and Emilie." She smiled at her son. "And I'm proud of you for the way you've stepped up to help them."

Matt blushed, and Nicole's heart did a somersault in her chest. Here was this big, strong lawman. Fierce. Independent. Powerful. And a kind word from his mother embarrassed him.

"Good night." Winnie led Walt out of the room.

Matt cleared his throat, and the color receded from his face. "I don't suppose you want to hear me second their opinion."

She dropped back onto the sofa. "I appreciate your family's hospitality. You all have been so kind, but I...I just can't stay here. Not with Grady in town."

Matt came to sit next to her. "My mom is right. I wish I could do more, but I'll pray for your safety."

His kindness sent tears pricking her eyes, and she wanted to trust in his goodness.

"Hey, hey." He searched her gaze. "What'd I say?"

"It's not you, it's me."

"How's that?"

She never wanted to discuss her failure, but for some reason, she felt compelled to explain it to Matt. "I want to trust you and in your kindness, but I can't. Not after Grady. I should never have dated him. He isn't a believer."

"Then why did you?"

"Hah!" she said. "That's the big question, isn't it? I wish I could say it was because he proved he was a good man. But it was his charm, plain and simple. He can be incredibly charismatic when he wants to be. And he came into my life at a time when I was lonely and vulnerable." She sighed. "Not that I'm trying to blame him. It was all my fault. The minute I learned he wasn't a believer, I should have told him I had no interest in dating him, but I didn't want to be alone. How pathetic is that?"

Matt held her gaze. "Not pathetic at all. God made us to need people."

"But I had—have—people in my life. Good people. Piper. Emilie. My family. I just missed having a man at my side. So I didn't even pray or ask God what I should do. I didn't have to. I knew what He would say. 'Don't yoke yourself to an unbeliever.' But I did what I wanted anyway. Now I'm paying the consequences, and God is extremely far away. I can't even feel Him in my life anymore."

She had to look away then as she couldn't bear to see disappointment in Matt's gaze.

He tucked a finger under her chin and turned her to face him. She wanted to pull away, but instead of disappointment or judgment she found understanding in his gaze. "I remember a situation like this in my own life. Not so long ago. I screwed up. Did what I wanted, even though I knew it was wrong. I felt guilty and tried to make up for it so God could love me again. Sadly, I never thought I'd done enough and all it did was separate me from Him even more. God gives us grace for when we mess up, and I should've just accepted it."

"I don't deserve His grace."

"But see…" Matt grabbed her hand and held it tightly. "That's what grace is all about. It's undeserved. His free gift."

Matt's intensity was over the top, and it was easy to see he really believed what he was saying. "All you have to do is ask for forgiveness for not listening. Let it go, and you'll feel God's presence again."

"I get that here." She stabbed a finger against her temple. "But in my heart? No. No. I don't get it there yet."

He nodded. "I wish I could help, but I know you have to reach that point on your own."

"But I hear you. Really, I do, and I promise to think about everything you said."

And she would. When they left tomorrow, she'd have plenty of time on the drive heading who knows where to think, and this topic would serve two purposes. It would help her work through the issue and would also give her something to keep her mind off this special man she was leaving behind.

EIGHT

Breakfast with Matt's family was a real joy, and despite Nicole's typical bad dreams of Grady the night before, she felt her mood lifting as they joked around. Along with her talk with Matt last night, they gave her hope that she could face her future. Let go of this thing with Grady. Be normal again. Have everything she'd once dreamed of.

She'd see if that held true when she went to bed that night in a town far from the McKades' ranch. As soon as she closed her eyes, would her worry be back in place? Grady's angry face filling her vision and telling her that she deserved nothing. Nothing at all.

Could she really grasp what Matt said last night? Not only know in her brain that she was forgiven, but embrace it in her heart? If nothing else, she might be able to take that away from her stay at Trails End.

When she couldn't sleep last night, she'd thought a lot about where she would go next. She'd first head to the bed-and-breakfast and if Grady was soon arrested and went to prison, she could go back to her apartment. If not, she would likely move home to her family in Minnesota. She would want Piper to come back with her as she was not only her sister but also her best friend.

Emilie swiveled on Matt's lap and peered up at him. "Will you take me out to see the horsies?"

Nicole hadn't told her daughter they were leaving today. Clem had said the car would be ready in the morning, but things happened, and she didn't want to tell Emilie they were taking off until it was a fact. She'd grown attached to the McKades, and it would be hard to leave.

Matt's phone rang, and he dug it from his pocket.

"Clem," he said and listened.

A deep frown took down his full lips, and Nicole couldn't help but think it was more bad news about her car. A moment of relief that maybe they'd be forced to stay another night warred with the knowledge that she was doing the right thing in running from Grady.

"Okay, be there soon." Matt's frown deepened as he stowed his phone.

"Is there a problem?" she asked and readied herself for his answer.

"Problem? Nah. Your car's ready. Clem's gonna take it for a quick test-drive around the block, but he said to head into town now, and it'll be ready by the time we get there."

"Oh, good," she said, but her heart ached with the thought, and she could hardly get her feet moving toward the door to walk away from Matt and the McKades forever.

Matt parked in front of Clem's garage and tried not to scowl. He hated this. Hated that he was taking Nicole to get the thing she needed to be able to walk out of his life. He didn't like it. Not one bit. But after talking to her last night, he knew she wasn't in a place to trust him when she didn't trust God. And it didn't seem like she would be able to let go of her issues anytime soon.

That meant he should give her even more space. But like a fool, he wanted to help her work through her problems, and that drew him closer to her. It didn't really matter, though, did it? This situation with Harmon was weighing heavy on her heart, and she needed to heal from the damage the jerk had inflicted before she could trust in God and other people again. Trust in him.

So even if he ever changed his stance on a relationship and wanted to date her, it would go nowhere. If it weren't for her safety, he knew it was better for her to leave now before he became fully invested in her and little Emilie, or she became attached to him, only for him to leave. Accepting that was a whole different story.

He shifted into Park and killed the engine. "Same procedure as yesterday. Straight inside."

She nodded, but he could see the confidence she'd tried to convey at the ranch was wavering. He squeezed her hand.

She clung to him and met his gaze. "Thank you again. I'll never forget your kindness."

He could get lost in those big blue eyes for, like, forever. He gave a quick nod and quickly got out of the car before he begged her not to leave him. He escorted her inside, and they found Clem standing next to the hoist that was holding up her car. A surprise to Matt as Clem had said the vehicle would be fixed by now. Maybe he'd run into a problem on the test-drive.

Did this mean Nicole wouldn't be leaving today? Matt felt ridiculously happy over the thought. He stepped into the garage. "Hey, Clem."

The older man spun, his gaze shooting around the space like a ricocheting bullet. "You scared me."

Matt saw Clem's hands shaking. Odd. This guy was usually laid-back and easygoing. The trembling raised

Matt's concerns, but Nicole stepped between him and Clem before he could ask about it.

"I thought my car would be fixed," she said.

"It was. I mean the alternator, that is. I was just going to call you about the other problem."

"Other?" Nicole's eyes narrowed. "I don't understand."

Clem shoved his hands into his coverall pockets. "It was running just fine until the test-drive. Before I could get very far, the car died again from something else."

"Oh, man," Nicole said. "So I won't be able to leave today?"

Clem shook his head. "And I think that's the least of your worries."

"How's that?" Matt asked, his concern building.

Clem removed a ball cap and slipped his fingers into graying hair, his hand still trembling. "Someone followed me on my test-drive. Can you believe that? He followed me. And then Nicole's car broke down and the guy took off."

Matt's radar went off, and he stood a step closer to Clem. "Followed, as in someone was tailing you?"

Clem bobbed his head. "As first I didn't think anything of it. Then after a few turns, I got suspicious. So I made a few more turns, and he didn't leave my bumper."

"Do you know who it was?" Nicole asked before Matt could ask the same question.

Clem clamped the cap back on and shook his head. "But I know my cars. It was a Chevy Tahoe. I caught the vehicle's license plate number, too."

Matt took out his notepad. "Give me the number."

Clem rattled it off, and Matt jotted it down.

"Color of the car?" Matt asked.

"White. A recent model, last few years."

"Give me a sec to call this in, and I'll see what I can

find out." Matt repeated the information into his radio for the dispatcher.

"Chevy Tahoe," the dispatcher said. "Registered to Hill Country Rentals out of Austin."

Say what? A rental car? Matt would get on the phone to the rental company and ask for the details, but he doubted they'd provide them without a warrant. What he could do right now was issue an alert, and he did before disconnecting and telling Nicole and Clem about Hill Country Rentals.

Nicole's gaze locked on his. "Do you think Grady was afraid I'd spot his truck and rented a car?"

"Likely." Matt took out his phone and showed Harmon's picture to Clem. "Could this be the man who followed you?"

Clem took the phone and held it out at arm's length. "Yeah. Yeah. Coulda been him. But everything happened so fast. I'm just not sure." He shoved the phone back into Matt's hands and looked like he'd seen something horrifying.

An overreaction as far as Matt was concerned for simply being followed, but Clem was a civilian and to him this was a big deal.

"I wish I coulda been positive about that." Clem met Matt's gaze and held it, fear firmly lodged in his eyes. "One thing I *am* certain of."

"What's that?" Matt asked.

"I'm not working on the car anymore."

"Why not?" Nicole cried out.

"First, we find the GPS tracker. Then I'm followed." He shook his head. "That's all bad enough, but then I find out the car was sabotaged."

NINE

"Sabotaged?" Nicole repeated while Matt's mind flew over the possibilities of what could have happened to her car.

She shot a look around as if she feared Harmon would step into the room any moment, and Matt resisted taking her hand in front of Clem.

"Explain, now," Matt demanded of Clem.

He tilted his head. "That's right. I didn't get that far, did I?"

"No." Matt tried not to let his anger over another troubling development get to him and upset Clem even more. He knew he hadn't managed it when Clem took a step back.

Clem clasped his hands together. "So like I said, the guy followed me and then the car broke down. I wasn't far from here and came back for the truck to tow the Accord back to the garage. With the way the thing came to a sudden stop and everything else that's happened, I kind of figured someone tampered with the car. That's when I looked for things that could take it down real fast."

"And you found something?" Nicole asked.

He nodded. "Someone filled your gas tank with sugar."

"Sugar?" Nicole asked. "But wouldn't that just melt in the gas?"

Clem shook his head. "No, but using sugar is one of the oldest tricks in the book. Not a big deal in the long run, but it'll stop the car dead until things are cleaned out."

"Could this have happened before I left Austin?" Nicole asked.

Clem shook his head. "You woulda never made it here if the sabotage had happened then."

"You keep the car inside or outside last night?" Matt asked.

"Inside, locked up tight. And I checked for signs of a break-in. Didn't find any."

Matt worked hard not to overreact to this news. He didn't want to alarm Nicole. "Must have happened when Nicole abandoned the car by the ranch. There haven't been any similar car tampering issues reported in the area. It must've—"

"Been Grady," Nicole finished for him, panic lodging on her face.

Clem tsked. "This guy sounds like a real piece of work. I don't want him anywhere near my business." He shifted to look at Nicole. "Sorry, miss, but like I said. I just can't work on the car anymore."

"Please," Nicole begged. "I need it. I have to leave. He's coming for me. I can't stay here and let him find me."

Clem looked around the room as if trying to find a better reason not to help Nicole, but his gaze softened. "I don't know."

She grabbed his arm and cast him a pleading look. Her expression resembled Emilie's begging expression, so much so that if they weren't facing such a serious development, Matt would have laughed.

"Grady could hurt me or my daughter," she said. "I can't stay in town. I just can't."

"Okay. Fine," Clem relented. "But if anything else happens before I get done with the car, I'm through. I won't risk my business and maybe even my life this way if that guy comes back."

"Thank you. Thank you. Thank you." Nicole threw her arms around Clem and hugged him. "How long before my car will be fixed?"

He blushed and pushed away. "I've got a couple cars I promised today, so not until late afternoon, if then."

"I understand."

Matt got that she really wanted to leave but now he was starting to think taking off was about more than protecting herself from Harmon. Was she also trying to run from God? Or was she trying to avoid the connection she seemed to have with Matt, and she was running from him, too?

That thought cut him to the quick. Sure, he didn't want a relationship, but he didn't like the thought that she found him so repugnant that she had to leave town.

"If you want that car today, I best be gettin' to work," Clem said. "I'll call when it's done."

"Thanks for all you're doing." Matt shook hands with the older gentleman and gestured at the door for Nicole.

They stepped out into the bright morning, the sun momentarily blinding Matt. He didn't like not being able to see well. He reached out for Nicole's arm, but she'd already moved ahead of him. She stood on the sidewalk, hand shielding her eyes, staring across the street.

He charged over to her. "What is it?"

She pointed across the street. "Near that door. I think it's Grady."

"In my car, now! I'll go talk to him." Matt stepped in

front of her, blocking her body from any attack by Harmon. Matt backed her to the car, careful to remain in front of her at all times. When he thought she should be opening the door, but didn't hear anything, he glanced back. She was just reaching for the handle.

The sound of a gunshot split the air.

Nicole. He spun, swept her into his arms and dove to the ground. On the way down, he saw Harmon duck away into an alley. Matt wanted to tear after the guy. Take him down and take him in. But he couldn't leave Nicole exposed. Nor could he risk trying to move her. He didn't see where the bullet had lodged but curved his body around her, his back to the shooter, and waited for Harmon to turn and fire another. Waited for a bullet to his back.

He grabbed his radio. "Shots fired. Backup needed."

Nicole was trembling in his arms, and her shaking worsened as he gave dispatch additional details, including their location.

"Deputy McKade, Kendall, is two blocks out," dispatch responded.

Matt acknowledged her response and released his mic. He tightened his hold on Nicole. "Hang in there, Nicole. Kendall's just around the corner. She'll be here soon."

"He shot at me," Nicole cried out. "Grady shot at me."

"Looks like it," was all Matt could think to say as there were no good words to use when confirming for someone that the person they'd once cared for had fired a bullet at them.

"How could he? I'm such a fool for ever trusting him. I'll never be able to trust my judgment again." She started crying, her body jerking with the sobs.

"Don't cry, honey." He drew her even closer, wishing he could remove all of her pain and anguish.

She fell silent. They lay there together. Time ticked by.

Matt heard a door groan open.

"Matt!" Clem yelled. "You okay?"

"Fine, Clem. Go back inside. Help's on the way."

Nicole started to get up.

"Not yet," Matt said. "Not until Kendall gets here."

"But I…we—"

"Don't worry. I've got you. You're fine." He wanted to add, *I'll always have your back*, but he couldn't make a promise like that when he knew she would leave Lost Creek.

The sound of a car taking off, the tires squealing, came from the north side of the street where Harmon had disappeared. Matt would dearly love to issue an alert for the car, but Matt had only heard a vehicle, not seen the make or model Harmon was driving. Still, if he was using a rental, there was already an alert out on that SUV, and now deputies would watch for it even more.

A vehicle came racing down the road, and Matt lifted his head to see a patrol car, lights flashing, speeding toward them. The deputy parked close by, blocking any future shots should Harmon still be in the area.

The door opened, and Kendall stepped out. "You two okay?"

"Fine." Matt reluctantly released his hold on Nicole. "Let's get you off the ground and inside the garage."

Matt knew Kendall would have his back, allowing him to get up and help Nicole to her feet. Her hands were as cold as icicles. Anger flared in his gut. How dare Harmon terrorize her like this?

He hurried her inside and took her into Clem's windowless office for protection. She dropped into a chair and started crying in earnest.

"Hey, hey." He squatted in front of her and whisked

away the tears with his thumb. "It's okay. I'm here. I won't let anything happen to you."

"How can you say that when Grady just shot at me?" Her voice rose.

He took her hands and made eye contact. "Because I'll take you back to the ranch. All the McKades will have your back 24/7. You can trust us. All of us." He'd let his vehemence take over, and his words came out far more forcefully than needed.

She jerked back.

Great. Now he'd scared her, too.

"I'm sorry. That was a little strong." He tightened his hold on her hands. "I only want what's best for you and Emilie. You know that, right?"

She opened her mouth to speak, but simply stared at him. He waited, breath held for her response. He'd settle for a simple yes. But she said nothing. She finally closed her mouth and looked away.

Matt's heart sliced in two. Never had anyone he cared about called his character into question like this. He suspected this came from her issues with Harmon, and Matt had been unable to convince her to trust him. And that meant, unless he figured out a way to overcome her fears before her car was fixed, she'd soon be ignoring his desire to help her and rushing off alone and into danger.

Nicole clung to Matt's hand and wanted to believe in his statement that he only wanted the best for her and Emilie, and she desperately wanted to believe in him. Not only because she'd been a sitting duck for Grady, and she needed Matt's protection until she could leave, but even more, because she was starting to have feelings for him.

How could that even be? She didn't trust him, and yet her heart was betraying her again. Had she not learned a thing from Grady? Here he was, shooting at her, and she wanted to give her heart to another man she didn't know anything about.

Craziness. Just plain craziness.

She extracted her hand, earning an exaggerated raise of Matt's eyebrows. So what? She'd be gone soon enough and these feelings growing between them would be in her rearview mirror just like the sweet little town of Lost Creek.

Clem stepped into his office, his eyes narrowed. "Was that the guy who followed me doin' the shooting?"

Matt came to his feet. "Likely."

Clem frowned and peered at Nicole. "Then I won't be working on your Accord. Gotta think of my customers and keep the danger away from this place. Soon as my mechanic gets in, I'll tow your car out to the ranch."

Nicole shot to her feet. "Please, Clem. No."

"Sorry, miss." Clem crossed his arms. "I won't cave this time." He turned and strode out of his office.

Nicole wanted to argue, but what could she say? He had a right to protect himself and his business. She had to figure out another way to get out of town today.

"Sit tight for a minute," Matt said, not looking at her. "I need to talk to Kendall, and then I'll take you back to the ranch."

Right, the ranch. She dropped onto the chair. She'd soon be back in the very place she wanted to leave. She had her wallet now and could take a bus or rent a car. Maybe the McKades would take her and Emilie to the bus stop or the closest car rental place. She'd ask Matt right now, but she was sure he'd say no, and she might fare better with the other members of his family.

She went to the door and the moment Matt entered the waiting area, she stepped out.

"We found the slug lodged in the garage wall. The shot was clearly meant for you." Seriously. It had happened. Grady had shot at her. Really shot at her.

And to think she'd almost brought Emilie along. Her child could have been shot. Could have died.

Oh, God, was that You keeping her safe? Are You still looking out for my precious child, even though I don't deserve Your care? Thank You. Thank You.

"Straight to the car," Matt said and took her arm to escort her outside.

She slipped into his patrol car. He joined her and as they pulled out of the lot, she searched the area, looking for Grady. He must really hate her if he'd been bold enough to take a shot at her with a deputy present. But then, he was the kind of guy who always believed he was right. Always perfect. Invincible, even.

She glanced at Matt. She'd think he was the same way, but she still hadn't learned enough about him to know.

And leaving town won't help you learn any more about him, either. Is that the way you want to live? Running from every man you meet?

She sat stunned at the thought that had come out of left field. She didn't want to spend her life running from anything, but she couldn't even consider what she wanted until this situation with Grady was resolved. If she ran, would it be resolved, though? Or would she always be looking over her shoulder?

Was she doing the right thing here, wanting to leave the McKades? To leave Matt?

He drove at a fast clip, his focus shifting to the mirrors at regular intervals like he feared another attack. And the moment they reached the ranch, he hurried her inside. His concern upped hers. Did he think Grady was nearby, gun at the ready?

Walt met them in the foyer. He ran his gaze over his son before switching his focus to her. She assumed he was looking for any injuries.

"So you're both okay?" A tremor rode through his tone, raising her anxiety even more.

She nodded, but her stomach roiled. If an unflappable man like Walt McKade was uneasy, she knew she should be shaking in her boots. Another confirmation that she needed to get far, far away from here.

"Come on in and sit down." He took Nicole's arm and led her to the family room, where Jed and Winnie waited on the sofa.

Winnie jumped up. Scooped Nicole into her arms for a hug, but soon released her to take hold of her son. "Praise God that neither of you were hurt."

She sat on the sofa, and Matt took what was seeming to be his usual position resting against the wall. He locked his focus on her, and she felt the intensity clear across the room.

She had to steel her resolve to find a way out of town. "You all have been so kind to us, but we need to go. There's got to be public transportation we could take, right? Like a bus, maybe?"

"Public transportation of *any* kind isn't an option, unless you want Harmon to track you," Matt said.

She hadn't thought of that. "You're right, but I still need to leave. I wouldn't ask this if I had another option, but I don't. Could I borrow a car from you all?"

"No!" The word erupted from Matt's mouth as he pushed from the wall and crossed his arms. "You're not leaving here and that's final."

"Son," Winnie said. "It's up to Nicole."

He took a step toward his mother. "You're right it is,

but it's up to us to decide if we'll lend her a car, and I'm forbidding that."

Walt eyed his son but didn't say a word.

"Fine, they're your cars." Matt lifted his hands in frustration. "You decide, but I won't stand here and watch you agree to it." He marched from the room and out the front door.

Nicole stared after him. Who was that man? He'd erupted like a blender without a lid.

Winnie faced Nicole. "I don't pretend to condone my son's rude behavior, but I think he's right about you not leaving. There's no need to leave when we can take care of you here."

"I agree," Walt said.

Nicole peered at Jed, and he crossed his arms. He was going to refuse her, too.

"Okay, I get it," she said. "I could rent a car, then."

"Austin's the closet place for that," Walt said. "And before you ask for a ride to Austin—"

"Don't," she finished for him.

"Exactly. That's also a good way for Harmon to track you."

Nicole reluctantly resigned herself to the fact that she was stuck here for now and had to make the best of it until she could figure out a safe way to leave.

The front door opened and closed. Matt stepped into the room. He looked calmer now, but when he moved toward her, she couldn't stop from pulling back.

He cringed and ran a hand over his thick hair. "Could I talk to Nicole alone, please?"

Without a word, his family members got up. On the way out of the room, Winnie squeezed his arm. Nicole saw a flash of emotions race across Matt's face, but he whisked them away before she could interpret them.

Once his family had departed, he moved closer to her. "Can I sit by you or do you think I'm a monster now?"

"Suit yourself."

Instead of sitting by her side, he perched on the coffee table and faced her. "I know I can't say anything that will make the way I exploded and got all bossy on you any better, but I am sorry."

She didn't know what to say so she said nothing at all.

"I don't usually have a temper." He clamped his hand on the back of his neck. "It's just, you being so all-fired eager to leave, when I know you're safer with me, got to me, and I blew up." He took a long shuddering breath. "I know you think I'm like Harmon. Like the way you now think most law enforcement officers behave, but I'm nothing like that. I would never hurt you. Physically or emotionally."

"You just did."

He planted his hands on his knees, his fingers going white. "I guess I can't pretend that I would never hurt your feelings. That's just unrealistic. But what I'm talking about is the deep emotional scar Harmon has left on you. That I would never do. Never. And I would try to never raise my voice to you again. My mother taught me better than that."

She believed him. Just like that. She believed him. He truly felt bad for his behavior.

"Can we forget it happened and start over?" He leaned closer.

She caught his unique minty scent that was becoming familiar to her now. She was tempted to give in. Let go of everything and let him take care of her. But she just wasn't ready for that.

"We can start over," she said, but she wouldn't let herself forget.

TEN

Minutes later, Matt heard his sisters arrive to discuss the investigation. Nicole said she needed some time to herself. He'd repaired the damage he'd done with her. At least as much as he could.

He'd handled situations that involved domestic abuse and violence, and he recognized the trauma she was going through, so he knew he had to proceed cautiously with her. But he believed she would still try to find a way to leave. She'd proven how tenacious she could be, and he doubted that she would give up.

He stepped into the dining room, where his sisters and mother had taken seats at the family's long dining table. His father, granddad and nana were missing, but he heard a mixer running in the kitchen, telling him Nana was still baking with Emilie. As to his dad, he didn't know, but it was odd that Granddad wasn't seated at the table, where a big plate of Nana's Christmas cookies sat in the middle and each person had a steaming mug of hot chocolate in front of them. Wasn't like Granddad to miss out on sweets of any kind.

He turned to go ask Nicole if she wanted cookies or cocoa and was surprised to see her joining them.

"Cocoa?" he asked.

"That sounds wonderful, but I can get it." She started for the kitchen door.

It swung open before she reached it, and Emilie came through. Her mouth and chin were covered in green icing. "Can I have a cookie, too, Mommy?"

Nicole's serious mood seemed to evaporate, and she smiled fondly at her daughter. "Looks like you might have already had one."

"Nuh-uh."

"Then how did you get frosting all over your face?"

She blinked her big eyes. "Nana let me lick the spoon and bowl, but I haven't had a cookie. Not one."

Nana joined them, a loving expression on her face and two mugs of hot chocolate in her hands for Matt and Nicole. "Emilie's right. A cookie hasn't touched the lips of this sweet child."

"See, Mommy. I told the truth." Emilie grinned. "Can I have a cookie now?"

"One," Nicole said.

Emilie climbed up on a chair and grabbed a Christmas tree with colorful sprinkles and icing to match the blobs on her face.

"You would choose the biggest one." Nicole chuckled.

An impish grin lit the child's face, and Matt didn't think there was a cuter child on earth.

"Bring your cookie in the kitchen," Nana said. "And I'll get a big glass of milk to go with it."

"Yay." Emilie scooted down and stopped by Matt's chair to look into his eyes. "Can Mommy and me stay here forever?"

"Emilie," Nicole said. "That's not a polite thing to ask."

"Why, Mommy?"

"It just isn't. Now scoot and eat your cookie."

She raised her big eyes back up to Matt. "Sorry for not being p'lite."

Matt couldn't resist that little face and scooped her up into his arms for a hug. She looked up at him. "I like you, Matt."

"I like you, too, munchkin."

She frowned. "I got frosting on your shirt."

"That's okay. It'll wash out."

"'kay." She wiggled free and skipped into the kitchen.

"She's so precious," Tessa said, surprising Matt.

His sister rarely thought of anything other than her forensics, but maybe now that she was engaged, she was considering having a family of her own. Matt wasn't even in a relationship, but it seemed like he hadn't stopped thinking about a family of his own since the Dyers walked into his life.

"I don't want to change the subject to something unpleasant," Kendall said, pulling Matt free of his thoughts. "But I'm due back on patrol in a few minutes, and we should talk about the shooting."

Matt didn't like seeing Nicole's good mood evaporate, but he was glad to leave his thoughts about her behind. "Did you locate anything in your neighborhood canvass?"

Kendall shook her head and looked at Nicole. "Are you positive the man you saw was Grady Harmon?"

"Yes."

"The guy *was* in the shadows." Matt cupped his mug, the warmth feeling good on the frosty, cold day. "Logically we can assume it was Harmon, but I couldn't testify to that fact."

Nicole set down her mug and eyed him. "I know what I saw."

Matt wanted to believe her, but witnesses were historically unreliable, and as a law enforcement officer, he had to remain skeptical. Still he wouldn't tell her that. She'd be offended, and he was already walking a tight-rope with her.

"Did you get a look at the gun, Matt?" Kendall asked.

Matt shook his head. "He wasn't holding a gun at first. I'm sure of that. But when I was moving Nicole to the car, I glanced back to check on her progress. The guy could have drawn and raised a weapon then, I suppose."

"What about you, Nicole?" Tessa asked. "Did you see a gun?"

She shook her head.

"I recovered the slug and calculated the trajectory," Tessa said. "The bullet was fired from the location where you saw the suspect. No question about that."

"Did you recover any casings?" Matt asked.

"Nah, the guy policed his brass."

Matt nodded. "Could be even more of a reason to believe it was Harmon. He'd never leave his brass behind."

"What does 'police his brass' even mean?" Nicole asked.

"He picked up the casing from the bullet he fired," Tessa replied. "Something a cop would know to do to stop us from analyzing it or even lifting prints from it."

"Oh."

Kendall leaned forward. "Matt, you said this guy was in the shadows. Do you think there could've been someone else with him?"

"It's possible, I suppose," Matt said, mulling over the thought. "But that would mean someone else wanted to kill Nicole."

"But who?" she cried out. "I don't live the kind of life where people are out to kill me."

Tessa grabbed a star-shaped cookie. "It could be the

guy Harmon either fired at in the motel or who shot at him."

"And again, I say—" Nicole ran her gaze around the group "—I don't have multiple people gunning for me."

"You're probably right." Kendall smiled, looking a lot like a younger version of their mother. "Harmon is our most likely suspect. We have the alert out on the rental car. Hopefully, he's actually driving that vehicle, and we'll pull him over."

Matt envisioned the guy coolly cruising in his rental car. His gun strapped at his side, a smirk on his face, while Nicole was terrified for her life. Red glazed over Matt's eyes. Bright, angry, bullfighting red.

He shot to his feet, his hands curled at his sides to keep his anger in check and not scare Nicole again. "I'll try for a warrant on the rental car."

He couldn't miss the surprised looks on his sisters' faces. Sure, the warrant was a long shot, but with the shooting, he would still go for it. He had to. They had nothing else to go on, and he had to find this creep before he took another shot at Nicole. "I'll get started on it now."

Kendall stood. "I'll let you know if Harmon's picked up."

"And I'll get that slug to ballistics to be compared to the one we recovered at the motel." Tessa got up, too, before she reached for another cookie.

His sisters exited the room, and he faced Nicole. He worked doubly hard to erase any anger from his voice. "Will you be okay alone while I work on that warrant?"

"She won't be alone." His mother circled her arm around Nicole's shoulder. "We'll all keep an eye out for her."

If Matt didn't know any better, he'd say Nicole looked

content at the thought. Maybe she was content with his family, and he was the only one who put her on edge.

He left the room, the thought rumbling around in his head. It only served to raise his anger at Harmon.

In his father's study, Matt prepared the warrant information as fast as he could. He double-checked the paperwork and emailed it to the judge's clerk, marking it as urgent. He started to get up to leave, but he was still mad and there was no point in going back in the other room until he could do so calmly. As a bonus, maybe if he put some space between him and Nicole, she wouldn't be as eager to take off.

He'd stay here for now and search online for any information he could locate on Harmon. He entered the guy's name into a search engine, but all he found was a picture of him in an Austin newspaper. Matt stared at the photo taken at a school assembly. Matt hated to admit it, but Harmon was a good-looking guy in his uniform. Fit. Tall. A big smile for the camera. A perfect poster boy for his department. Matt read the story that gushed over Harmon's service, and all it did was send Matt's stomach churning with more anger.

When Matt hauled this guy in, and he went to trial for firing at a defenseless woman, all of Harmon's arrests would be called into question and put a smudge on the police department's reputation.

Matt sighed out a breath. He couldn't change that there were bad officers in the world today, other than being the best deputy he could be. When he became sheriff, he'd make sure that his deputies were the best as well.

He moved on to social media, and like Nicole had said, Harmon didn't have a presence there. Matt's email dinged, and he clicked on the message from the judge's clerk. Warrant denied. Not surprising. Matt couldn't be sure that it was Harmon who shot at Nicole, nor did he have any facts to connect the rental car to Harmon. But still, if Matt had to do it all over again, he would do the same.

The only option now was to call Hill Country Rentals. He located their phone number and dialed, then asked for the supervisor, and though she was pleasant enough, she turned his request down flat. No surprise there, either, but he still pounded a fist on the desk.

He heard the front door slam and booted footfalls heading his way. Matt jumped up and went to the door.

His dad stormed down the hall. "Of all the fool things to do."

"What?" Matt said, certain his father couldn't know about the warrant request yet.

"The fact that you have to ask is even worse. There are so many things wrong with your warrant request, I can hardly think straight."

"You heard?"

"Judge called me the minute it hit his desk. Asked if this is what he has to look forward to when I retire."

Matt cringed. "Granted, getting one for the rental car records was a long shot, but I had to do it. We have nothing else to go on."

"I taught you better." His father stepped closer, going toe-to-toe with him. "You're letting your interest in Nicole cloud your good sense. One more stunt like this, and I'll insist you step away from the investigation."

"Come on, Dad. It's not that bad. We often request warrants that are turned down."

"Yes, but not because we lost our senses. If you keep this up, you'll soon convince the judges and your fellow deputies that you have no business running for sheriff."

Matt stepped back and ran a hand over his face. He

hadn't thought of what his request might mean long-term. All he'd thought about was the gunshot that could have taken Nicole's life, and he'd seen red. He'd told her that he didn't have a temper, but honestly, he was developing one because he couldn't go very long without losing his cool when it came to threats made to her life.

"If you can't do a better job of controlling yourself, you should let Kendall take over," his dad added.

The thought of letting his sister take charge because he couldn't do his job left him feeling nauseated. He'd never botched things up on the job. Never. It was time he faced facts. Nicole and Emilie had come to mean a lot to him, and he had to find a way to deal with those feelings or risk ruining his future career that meant everything to him.

"I've got this," he said and tried to sound in control when his body was nearly exploding with conflicting emotions.

His dad eyed him for a long time as if trying to decide if he could trust Matt. "What's your next move?"

"To call Harmon's supervisor. Maybe he can give us something to go on."

"I wondered why you didn't do that already."

"I didn't want anyone to alert Harmon of our interest in him and potentially hinder the investigation."

"So why do it now?"

Matt didn't answer his father. What could he say? Desperate times called for desperate measures? His father wouldn't like hearing that Matt was desperate. He didn't like it much himself, and he had to find a way to control it and do right by Nicole and Emilie.

"Seeing's how you're not gonna answer me, you can bring me up to speed on what's happened today."

Matt filled him in on his meeting with his sisters.

His father ground his teeth. "So why disable a car that was already disabled?"

"Maybe Harmon figured that the sugar would keep her here longer."

"Then he wants Nicole to remain in Lost Creek."

"But why?" Matt asked. "He likely has no idea we found the tracker, and he'd rather she used her car than a rental, right?"

"Could be," his dad replied. "Or it might not have anything to with being able to track her in the future. He might not know she filed a report on the knife and thinks if she returns to Austin and reports it, that he'll be found guilty of breaking into her apartment and violating his restraining order."

"He could be trying to stop her from doing that," Matt said, his mind running through other scenarios. "Or worse, he might think we don't know he's in town, and he can kill her here and hide her body. *And* hope a murder this far from Austin would never be connected to him."

Nicole had heard Matt and his father arguing all the way in the kitchen, where she was cutting out sugar cookies with Emilie. It had felt wrong to join his mother and nana to bake cookies when Grady was trying to end her life, but she had nothing else to do, and she was glad for the opportunity to spend this time with Emilie doing something special for Christmas.

They'd planned a full week of events. They would bake their own cookies. Make cards. A gingerbread house. Watch old Christmas cartoons. Now they were on the run for their lives.

Nicole let out all her frustrations in a long sigh.

Betty looked up from her rolling pin. "You look worried."

"Matt and his dad," she said, keeping the focus on them instead of her.

Betty shook her head. "I heard them."

"Would be hard not to." Winnie frowned. "I wish I could say it never happens, but Walt's a real taskmaster when it comes to work. He's been a good role model for our children, but there are times I wish he would go lighter on them."

Nicole thought about her own family. "My dad's like that with my brothers, but I have to say he spoils me and my sister."

Emilie looked up, her nose covered in flour. "And me."

Nicole smiled at her daughter. "Yes, you, too."

"Walt does worry about the girls more, though," Betty said. "I know it drives them both crazy."

Winnie sighed. "That he does."

With the stress, Nicole had lost all interest in the cookie baking. "Would you mind if I went to see if it's more than that and anything else has come up?"

Betty waved her floury hand. "Go ahead."

"Yeah, Mommy. It's okay. Nana knows everything about baking."

"She does, does she?" Nicole ruffled Emilie's hair. "Sounds like I'm quickly being replaced."

"I'd never dream of it." Betty's eyes twinkled. "But I would dream of having this little one around here on a regular basis."

Nicole gaped at her.

"What?" She winked. "An old woman without any great-grandchildren can hope, right?"

Nicole didn't have a clue how to respond, so she slipped out of the room. By the time she reached Walt's office, Matt was gone, and Walt sat behind his desk.

He looked up. "Help you?"

She didn't know if she should mention the argument, but she had to know what was going on, so she nodded. "I heard you and Matt."

"Sorry about that." He ran his finger over his mustache. "I was a little hard on him."

"Did he do something wrong?"

"Nothing we can't overcome."

She could tell he didn't plan to explain it to her, and she wouldn't keep asking. But she did have to wonder if his unwillingness to discuss it was because he was keeping something from her. If so, she had to know what, and Matt might tell her. "Where'd Matt go?"

"For a ride. You'll likely find him down at the corral saddling up Ranger."

"Thanks," she said and headed for the front door. She grabbed her jacket and stepped outside. She tried to shrug into her coat, but the wind caught it, dragging her across the porch. She finally wrangled control of it and got it zipped up.

Head down, she hurried across the yard. The last thing she wanted was to go near a horse, but she had to know if something else had happened and be prepared. Not finding Matt in the corral, she opened the big door to the barn and stepped inside. A large light shone overhead, and the smells of straw and horses met her nose. Matt stood in the middle of the room with stalls lining both walls. He hefted a saddle up on the largest horse she'd ever seen. He was a glossy black and looked fiercely independent standing there eyeing her. There was no fence or barrier between her and the horse, and her knees felt weak.

"I didn't expect to see you here." Matt met her gaze, but a shadow from his cowboy hat hid his eyes, and she couldn't read his mood. "Come meet Ranger."

"No. No." She backed away.

He tightened the strap that held the saddle on his back. "He's not as fierce as he looks."

As if on cue, the horse tossed back his head and whinnied.

"He's putting on a show for you and trying to make you think he's hot stuff." Matt chuckled.

She couldn't laugh and moved a few more steps back.

Matt left the horse and came over to her.

"Shouldn't you be watching him?" she asked.

"He really does have good manners, and he'll be fine." Matt held out his hand. "C'mon. He's easygoing. I promise."

She bit her lip and stared at him.

"Do it for Emilie. She'd be proud to see you overcome your fear."

Nicole frowned at him. "It's not fair, bringing her into this."

"I know." His mouth tipped up in a lopsided boyish grin as he tilted his hat back, showing her a fun side to his personality that she hadn't experienced.

And wow! He was amazing to look at, standing there all cowboy-like in his jeans, denim jacket and boots. She could hardly keep from smiling back at him, and she couldn't resist taking his hand. It was warm and calloused, and her heart nearly burst from his touch.

He pulled her closer, his smile disappearing as his gaze sought hers and locked in a powerful hold. She was helpless to pull away and simply stood looking up at him. She was close enough to see each individual whisker on his chin, and a faint scar on his cheek that she hadn't noticed before. She lifted her free hand and ran her finger over it.

He inhaled a quick breath.

"How did you get this scar?" she asked, barely able to speak.

"Fell off my horse."

"What?" She snapped back. "And you're trying to get me to meet him?"

"Just kidding. A suspect hit me with a board." He chuckled.

She shook her head but laughed with him. She could easily get used to this. Emilie in the kitchen with amazing women. Her with a man she could count on. Wait, what? She was thinking she could count on him now? When did that happen?"

He tapped her forehead. "What's going on in there? You went from having a good time to worried in a flash."

"It's nothing. I should be heading back to the house."

"You must've had a reason for coming out here."

"I heard you and your dad arguing. I wondered if there was anything new on Grady."

Matt shook his head. "My dad was taking me to task for requesting the warrant for the rental car records."

"Why would he do that?"

"Because I didn't have any probable cause and shouldn't have done so. Now the judge is wondering what kind of sheriff I would be." He shook his head. "I just wasn't thinking."

"Why not?"

"You." He gently cupped the side of her face. "You do something to me, and I can't think straight."

Every instinct in her body said to step away before she found herself involved with another man she wasn't sure she could trust, but her heart had her leaning into the warmth of his hand.

"Nicole, I…"

"Shh," she said and wrapped a hand around his neck to bring his head down for a kiss.

She was shocked at her forward behavior, but she wanted more than a simple touch. His lips settled on hers. She pressed closer and reveled in the pure touch of his lips on hers. He slid his hand around her waist and drew her in tight. His free hand went around her other side, and she could hardly breathe for how close he was holding her.

She had wondered how it would feel to let this big, tough cowboy hold her. Now she knew, and her expectations paled in comparison to the reality of it. The kiss deepened, but suddenly he was jolted forward, taking her with him for a tumble into a bed of straw.

He shifted off her, and a big black horse head bent over her. She gasped and tried to scramble away.

Matt held her in place. "Not cool head-butting me, Ranger. But as long as you're here, meet Nicole."

"I…" she said, searching for the right words with that massive head leaning even closer. "I need to go."

"Hang on," Matt said. "He won't hurt you."

"I know," she said and honestly believed him.

But reality had set in and this man, this handsome cowboy with one arm still around her back, could hurt her. Very badly. And after that kiss, she knew just how much.

ELEVEN

Sunday breakfast was a typical affair after church, with Nana in the kitchen cooking up a storm and the family talking about their day and the next morning was no exception. What wasn't normal was the tiny person sitting on Matt's lap again, stabbing scrambled eggs with a kid's fork that his nana had rustled up from somewhere. And Nicole wearing a dress she borrowed from his sister, sitting across from him, her hair pulled back in a neat bun emphasizing her big eyes.

They'd considered the risk of attending church, but with Gavin and Kendall going as an advance team and scoping out the area, and then the rest of the McKades securely transporting Nicole, they decided it was safe enough to go. They followed the reverse procedure coming home.

Emilie wiggled, drawing Matt's attention. Nicole had offered to hold her daughter, but Emilie had insisted on sitting with him. She again said she liked him and despite that bringing a frown to Nicole's face, Matt's heart warmed over the child's declaration.

His phone rang, and he shifted Emilie to get it out of his pocket. When he saw it was Harmon's lieutenant calling back, Matt stood and set Emilie on the chair. "Gotta answer this, sweetheart."

"'kay." She went back to eating, reaching high to get to her plate.

"Excuse me," he told the others and hurried from the room, answering as he walked.

"What can I do for you, Deputy?" Lieutenant Ackerson asked.

"I'm interested in getting information on Grady Harmon."

A long sigh came from the phone. "Let me tell you right up front—I won't share much information about one of my officers."

"Your commitment to your people is commendable, but I have quite a situation here and need to find Harmon." Matt explained what had been happening, making sure to keep from mentioning where Nicole was staying so it couldn't get back to Harmon.

Ackerson let out another heavy breath. "Go ahead and ask your questions, and I'll decide if I want to answer."

"Fair enough." Matt stepped into his dad's study and went to the window overlooking the backyard. "Is Harmon on the job now?"

"I haven't seen him for a few days."

"He called off sick?"

"No."

"So he's AWOL," Matt stated.

"Your word, not mine."

Translated, that meant, yeah, the guy had not shown up for work. "Tell me about his state of mind before he took off."

"What about it?"

"Was Harmon happy?" he asked.

"Happy?" Ackerson asked. "What officer is happy on

the job? It's a life-or-death position, you know that. Happiness isn't something I look for."

"Maybe happy isn't the right word. Content."

"Not so much."

"Did he share what was bothering him?"

"Not so much."

Matt curled his hand in frustration. "I know he had a job outside of work and officers have to report companies they work for outside the force. Can you give me the name of his employer?"

"Not so much."

His repeated usage of those three words was raising Matt's ire, but he should just be glad the guy agreed to answer any questions. "But he does work as a security guard in his off hours?"

"Yeah."

"Know if it's for a firm or an independent gig?"

"Don't remember."

At least Matt finally got a few different answers. "You said he didn't seem content. Do you think it has to do with the fact that he broke up with his girlfriend?"

"Could be."

"And what do you think about the restraining order she filed?"

"It's bogus." He snapped out the words. "The chick is lying, but you know how judges side with potential victims these days. Even if the order isn't really necessary."

"That's a good thing, don't you think? Keeps women in difficult situations safer."

"For the most part, but it can also ruin a man's life if she goes off on him and files out of spite, like this one."

"You don't seem willing to think your officer is capable of stalking this woman."

"Look," Ackerman said. "I don't know you from

Adam. You call and act like you want to prove one of my guys is up to no good. But Harmon's a good officer. No problems on the job. No disciplinary actions. A solid cop."

"But we're not really talking about what he does on the job, are we? It's what he's doing off the job."

"Something I don't have anything to say about." He fell silent for a moment.

Matt wouldn't risk him hanging up before he got all of his questions answered. "I've put in a request for blotter information regarding Harmon violating the RO a few days ago, but I still haven't received it."

"I can look into that for you," he said, but he sounded about as willing to send the information as the sergeant Kendall had spoken to. Not that it really mattered anymore. Matt believed Nicole.

"Now if you'll excuse me," Ackerman said, "I have work to do."

"Would you let me know if you hear from him?"

"I'll tell him to call you. That's the best I can do." Ackerman disconnected.

Matt turned and found Nicole standing outside the office door.

"That was Harmon's lieutenant," he told her as he pocketed his phone.

"Did he tell you anything to help?"

"Not really. Said Harmon was AWOL from work for a few days, which helps confirm he's here. Also said he'd been discontented, but he didn't know about what. I brought up your breakup and the restraining order."

"And let me guess, he's on Grady's side."

Matt nodded. "It's a touchy thing, you know? He said Harmon was a great cop, but that doesn't mean he's not a real jerk off the job."

She didn't say anything for a long time, but simply watched him, her eyes narrowing. "You believe me, though, don't you?"

"Yes, of course."

"Thank you." She seemed to want to say more but didn't speak. He wanted to hear her response and resisted the urge to say anything.

"I'm so sorry for disrupting your life like this," she said.

"No worries," he replied, though she had no idea how much she'd disrupted things.

Case in point, he wanted to pull her close and kiss her again. And more. Maybe ask her to stay in town, and they could what? Start dating? His priorities hadn't changed. He couldn't risk letting his family down. Or letting himself down by not achieving his dream job. No matter the feelings he was starting to develop for this amazing woman.

His phone rang. He glanced at the screen and quickly answered. "Dad."

"A body's been found near the motel. Guy died of a gunshot wound. No identification, but he fits Harmon's description."

"I'm on my way." Matt tried to hide his shock and shoved his phone into his pocket.

Nicole met his gaze. "What happened?"

"A man was gunned down by the motel. Dad says he doesn't have ID, but he fits Harmon's description."

Nicole's eyes went wide, and she clutched her chest. "Do you really think it's Grady?"

"I don't know, but I aim to find out." Matt was eager to take off, but he had to think about Nicole's safety before going. "I need you to stay here with Granddad. Can you promise me you'll do that and not leave the property for any reason?"

"Yes…yes, of course." Her eyes filled with panic.

He didn't like seeing it and wished he could stay, but he couldn't. He swept her into his arms and held her tight. Her arms went around his back, shocking him when she drew him even closer and nestled her head against his shoulder.

"It'll be okay, honey," he whispered against her soft hair. "I promise."

"How can you promise that after a man has been murdered?"

He leaned back. "Because I'd die before I let anything happen to you or Emilie. Just know that."

"I do," she said, but she sounded so sad it broke his heart.

He wanted to delve into the reason, but he had to leave. He needed to know if Harmon was dead, and he needed to know now. "We don't know for sure that the victim is Harmon, so I'll tell Granddad on the way out that I'm going. He's older, but he's still very capable. You can count on him."

She nodded, and he broke contact, immediately missing the feel of her in his arms. He raced to the kitchen and updated his granddad before rushing out to his patrol car, turning the lights and siren on before he hit the end of the driveway.

He soon pulled up to the field behind the motel. His father's car was parked at the edge of the wide-open area next to another patrol vehicle. As much as he didn't want Kendall to have to see a murder victim, he hoped she was the first responder. She would've properly secured the scene and a less experienced deputy might not be as careful, allowing evidence to be destroyed.

He parked by his dad's car and jumped from the vehicle. He wanted to jog across the big field, but after the earlier conversation with his dad, Matt wouldn't arrive out of breath and acting like a madman.

He surveyed the area ahead and saw several paths of trampled grass leading to his father.

"Take the path on the far right," his father called out.

Matt headed into the field on the designated route. With each step, he tried to heed his warning to chill out, but all he could think about was that he might see Harmon in a moment, and Nicole's problems could be over. Meant she would leave and take Emilie with her. The thought of not seeing them cut through him like the blade of the ax he used to chop firewood.

As he approached his dad, he saw Kendall was indeed the deputy staring down at knee-high grass. Matt had to assume the victim was laying in front of her.

His father turned, holding a cell phone. "Guy might be the right size and build, but he doesn't look like the picture Kendall shared."

Matt had memorized every one of Harmon's facial features from the pictures he'd seen of Harmon and could easily determine if the deceased was indeed the man terrorizing Nicole. Matt's gaze went straight to the guy's face. He took in the high forehead, wide jaw and long face. "You're right. It's not Harmon."

Emotions warred in his gut. Nicole wasn't safe yet. "What do we have so far?"

"Zeke reported hearing a gunshot," Kendall said. "I responded, wondering if we had another discharge in the motel. He said it had come from this area. I did a grid search and found the body. Shooter was long gone."

Matt squatted by the body and took a picture of his

face. "Powder burns around the entrance wound suggests he was shot at close range."

"My thoughts, too," his father said. "I've called the ME. Once she gets here, we can search the body for ID."

Matt didn't want to wait for the medical examiner, but they couldn't touch the victim until authorized to do so. Or before crime scene photos were taken.

Matt stared at the guy's face. Who was this man? Might his death be related to Harmon or was it just a co-incidence? Matt didn't believe in coincidences, and with the few murders that occurred in Lost Creek, he had to think a connection existed.

He stood. "We need to get forensics out here."

"Already on the way," his dad replied.

Kendall pointed a few feet away at the paths. "We have a clear entrance and exit path from the scene."

"We need to get this scene cordoned off," Matt said.

"I'll grab the tape and some stakes." Kendall took off for her vehicle.

Matt peered at his father. "Has anyone questioned Zeke yet?"

"Kendall talked to him about hearing the shot, but she hasn't left the body since she found him."

"Then I'll go do that while you two secure the scene." Matt waited for his father to argue, as securing a scene was a basic patrol task not often handled by the sheriff.

"You can go, *after* Kendall drops off the stakes and tape. I'll handle the scene, and you can take her with you. If she hopes to be half the detective you are, she needs to start shadowing you."

Matt felt his shoulders rising under his father's compliment. They were few and far between and he had to savor every one of them. Especially after the dressing-down he'd received earlier.

Kendall returned and set down the supplies near one of the paths. His dad joined her. "Matt's going to question Zeke. I want you to go with him and observe."

Her eyebrow rose, making her look the spitting image of their mother, and Matt didn't know how his dad handled it. Matt started for the motel and heard the dried grass swishing behind him as Kendall followed.

"Can you believe this?" she asked in the parking lot.

He glanced at her. "You mean a murder in Lost Creek?"

"No. Dad staking the site. I have half a mind to turn around and record it with my phone." She chuckled.

Matt wished he could find some humor, but if this murder was connected to Harmon, it meant Nicole's life was in even more danger.

"Hey, man," Kendall said. "Lighten up or you're going to stroke out."

She was right. It was common for law enforcement officers to handle the stress of such a tragedy by cracking jokes, but handle the stress of Nicole's life in danger that way? No. That wasn't even possible.

Kendall grabbed his arm and forced him to look at her. "It's Nicole, isn't it?"

"I don't know what you mean."

"Oh, yeah, you do. You've fallen for her. I can see why. She's gorgeous and sweet. And Emilie. Can you imagine having such a cutie-pie as your own?"

Yeah, he could. Easily. And that made him pick up speed.

"You can't run away from how you're feeling," she called after him, and he heard her footsteps as she hurried to catch up to him.

He glanced at her. "I'm actually surprised at your comment. I thought we understood each other in ways the others couldn't."

She searched his gaze. "You mean about the job coming first until we realize our goals?"

"Exactly. And I have a lot of work to do before I get elected." He picked up speed again.

"I hear you, bro. I can't let up, either. It'll take some convincing to get Dad to give me your detective slot. Especially with Braden on the force now." Tessa's fiancé was a former Houston PD detective. When he got engaged to Tessa, he joined their team as a patrol deputy, but his detective skills made him the most logical deputy to step into the position that would become vacant if Matt moved up to sheriff.

"It's no secret that Braden wants a detective's position, but he knows you're up for this slot and won't even put his name in the running."

"Doesn't mean Dad doesn't want him in the job." She shot him a look. "But this isn't about me, and it isn't even about your skills for the sheriff's position. It's about being popular to gain votes. Having a wife and child wouldn't hurt those chances."

He spun on her. "And then what? I get the job, and I work from sunrise to sundown. Maybe longer. Seven days a week. How would that be fair to Nicole or Emilie?"

"You can set your own hours."

"Right, and I will. Long ones, if I aim to be as good as Dad and Granddad in the job."

"I think you're forgetting. They aren't perfect and didn't start out knowing the job inside and out. It took time."

"And the more I work, the sooner I'll put in that time." He turned to end the discussion and marched into the motel lobby.

Zeke stood behind the counter. Nearly six feet, he was

as thin as a broomstick, and he had a full beard of dark gray whiskers. "You find the shooter?"

Matt shook his head. "But we found a victim."

Zeke's weatherworn face paled. "Someone was shot?"

"Murdered, actually." Matt came right out with it as there was no easy way to tell someone about a violent death.

"Who?" The word eased out of Zeke's mouth on a strangled breath.

"Don't know yet." Matt scrolled on his phone to the photo of the deceased. "I wish I didn't have to show you the victim's picture, but I'm hoping you can help us ID him."

Zeke pushed up black-rimmed glasses and took a quick look, his color receding even more. "I don't know his name, but he stopped by here yesterday. He asked about that Grady Harmon fella. 'Course, I didn't know his name then, but the guy showed me Harmon's picture, and I confirmed he was staying here."

"What?" Matt's voice hit the ceiling. "Why didn't you tell us about this when I questioned you before?"

"The guy flashed an Austin police badge. I figured he was working with you all, and he'd have told you about the conversation."

"You thought I was working with another agency?" Matt clarified.

"Yeah, I mean, I didn't really have time to give it a lot of thought. It was checkout time, and I was swamped. He flashed a picture on his phone like you did and asked if the guy was a guest. I said yes. That was it. He didn't even ask for the room number or mention his name."

Matt couldn't chastise Zeke for failing to mention the visit. He couldn't have known the man wasn't a cop and that he would be murdered. Or for that matter, even have known that Harmon wasn't Otto Cutler like he claimed and was terrorizing Nicole. "Did you ever see him again?"

"Nah, just the one time. After I said Harmon was staying here, he put away his badge and took off."

"Did you see the man's name on his credentials?"

Zeke cringed and pushed his glasses up his nose. "Like I said, I was busy. Didn't look too closely."

Matt had to consider that the deceased worked with Harmon and could actually be another police officer. If this guy really was a cop, when the ME took prints from the body, they'd find a match in the database.

"Thanks, Zeke. Appreciate your help." Matt gestured for Kendall to depart.

They stepped outside in time to see the ME's van pull into the lot.

Kendall stopped to stare at the vehicle. "Do you think we're really looking at a murdered police officer?"

"Could be."

She continued to stare at the vehicle. "It's seeming likely to me. I mean, it makes sense that Harmon could've had a beef with one of his coworkers."

"True that." Matt headed straight for the ME's van, thinking how his conversation with the lieutenant about Harmon's discontent gave credence to their theory. "And we're about to find out if you're right."

TWELVE

"So his prints aren't in the database and he has no ID." Matt got up from searching the deceased's pockets. "Thankfully the ME has a portable scanner to take his prints on scene so we already know he wasn't a law enforcement officer."

"I can't believe I was buying into that." Kendall met Matt's gaze.

"The thing is, sis," Matt said, "what your gut says in an investigation isn't important without evidence to back it up. Sure, you can follow your gut to investigate, but don't use your suspicions to form a theory. If you do, you'll work hard to prove your theory and close your mind to other possibilities."

She eyed him. "Don't tell me you weren't thinking the same thing."

"Sure, I thought it was possible, but I didn't buy into it the way you did."

"I've got a lot to learn, I guess." She frowned.

"Hey," he said. "We all started where you are. As a patrol deputy, you have to go on what you see and often react quickly based on that. But as a detective, you have to dig for evidence to support everything."

She nodded but looked a bit frustrated. "Where do we go from here?"

"The autopsy." He stepped over to the ME, Alicia Wagner, who was loading the body on a gurney with the morgue assistant's help. "I need the slug ASAP to compare to others recovered in recent shootings."

"You need." She planted her hands on her waist, cinching the oversize Tyvek suit. "So does everyone else."

He didn't back down under her pointed stare. "I know you're busy, Doc, but John Doe has to take priority in your schedule."

"Says you."

Matt resisted, frowning. "Do any of your other cases involve finding a murderer before he kills again?"

She sighed and held his gaze for another beat before grabbing the gurney. "I'll start the procedure the minute we get back to the morgue."

"Thank you," Matt said.

She raised an eyebrow above her protective glasses. "You'll owe me."

Matt nodded. He hated owing favors, but this one was definitely worth it if it led them to Harmon, who now appeared to also be a murderer. Sure, Matt had no facts to support that theory. Just his gut feel, and as he warned Kendall, he had to keep an open mind and wait for the facts before he could take action.

He crossed over to Tessa, who'd carried her many equipment cases out to the field and now squatted near one of the paths. She studied something on the ground, and he had to shake his head at the sight of his baby sister at a crime scene. She stopped growing in high school, topping off at five-feet-four inches. Her stature along with her cute smile and freckles left him and other family members still thinking of her as a kid, despite the fact that she was in her thirties and a very accomplished investigator.

He stopped next to her. "ME's gonna do the autopsy right away. I'll pick the slug up from her. The firearms experts can examine the rifling and compare to the other bullets."

"Okay," she said without looking up.

"This is our top priority right now, and I need you to sit on the firearms staff until they get it done. Understood?"

She picked something up with tweezers and peered at it. "Yeah, I got it."

"I'm heading back to the ranch to show John Doe's picture to Nicole. Keep me updated on anything you find."

She nodded, but still kept her focus on the object. She was often in her own world when working her job, and he could only hope that she'd really heard him. He shared his plans with Kendall, too, and then started across the field. Reporters and lookie-loos stood at the road, calling out questions to him. He went on autopilot and said, "No comment," leaving the public relations to his father.

But as Matt started down the road in his patrol car, he realized that, if he was elected sheriff, it would be his job to talk to the press. He didn't look forward to that aspect of the job. Not that he didn't think he could do it and do it well, but he didn't have any experience with it. He needed to talk to his father and start learning from him.

There was so much to grasp about the sheriff's job. Press, budgets, supervision, procedures, personnel reviews and protocols. He was like Kendall, a greenhorn, and until he wasn't, he needed to be hands-on in every aspect.

He'd gotten sidetracked a bit with Nicole and Emilie, but it was time to get back on track. The people of Lake County could count on him doing his best for them. No matter what it took.

What about trusting God to have your back instead?

Where'd that come from? Matt believed in God. Even

trusted Him for most things in his life, but this? Nah, he had to do more than just trust God. Matt had to take charge like his dad had taught him. Make his own path. Make things happen.

He pulled up to the ranch. His phone dinged, signaling an email. He glanced at the screen to see he'd received the historical call log from Harmon's phone. Perfect timing. He'd do a reverse phone lookup to determine the identity of people Harmon had talked to, and maybe that would give them John Doe's identity.

He exited the car, pulling his jacket closed against the brisk wind. Seemed like it had gotten colder in the last few years, and there was no such thing as normal weather anymore. Or maybe as he got older he just didn't like the cold as much.

He climbed the steps two at a time, barely noticing the wreathes and fresh garland decorating the long porch. He'd seen the same sight at Christmastime for as long as he could remember, and it always made him remember the real reason for the season as his parents always brought that home by telling Bible stories as they put up the Christmas decorations. He pushed the door open, the heat a blessing.

Emilie came running toward him, a snowman-shaped dough ornament in her hand. She smiled up at him, her eyes crinkling. She lifted her arms up to him, and he forgot all about the murder. About the danger outside. About everything but the pure joy of a child happy to see him. He picked her up.

She held out her ornament. "I want to hang mine right next to yours."

He leaned close to the tree, allowing her to reach it, and wondered why she was alone.

She slipped the ribbon over a branch, and her varnished snowman swung into place next to his. "Mommy still doesn't know about hers. Nana said we can hang it up on Christmas Day."

What was his nana thinking? Christmas Eve was tomorrow, and there was always a possibility that they wouldn't still be at the ranch. Nana should know not to get this child's hopes up.

Emilie pushed the snowman, sending it swinging on the branch. "Nana said she'd help me make presents for everyone."

"That's my nana. Always helpful."

Emilie clasped her hands on both sides of his face and brought her forehead to rest on his like he'd seen her do with her mother. "Don't tell anyone. I prayed for a daddy for Christmas. A daddy like you."

Emotions swam through Matt's gut, tangling with everything that had transpired since she'd burst into his life like a breath of fresh air.

Matt wanted to warn her that he wasn't ready to be a father, but there was no way he would break her heart. "Where's your mommy?"

"She has a headache. She's resting." Emilie squirmed free and scampered toward the kitchen, where the sound of pans clanking echoed through the house. "We're making gingerbread men today."

She disappeared through the swinging door, and Matt turned to the stairway. Nicole stood at the top, a frown on her face, and she tightly clutched the banister, her fingers turning white. She was clearly upset about something. If she'd been standing there long enough, she'd overheard his conversation with Emilie, and he could see how that would make her frown.

"I guess you heard Emilie's prayer," he said.

"I did." She released the banister and started down the stairs. "I'll have to tell her that won't happen."

Matt nodded, but he could already visualize Emilie's disappointed expression, and he wished the little princess didn't have to go through that. But then, that's how kids learned. He just didn't want his favorite little girl to have to learn those hard lessons.

Nicole stopped on the second step and rested against the newel post. "Was Grady murdered?"

Matt shook his head.

"So someone else died." She kept her voice low and Matt had to assume that, even with the kitchen door closed, Nicole was worried about Emilie overhearing. "I'm such a horrible person. I was honestly hoping it was Grady."

"I thought the same thing." He took her hand. "C'mon. Let's sit down. I have something to show you."

Her eyes widened. "That sounds bad."

He didn't respond but led her to the sofa, where he sat next to her. He took out his phone. "This isn't pretty. It's a picture of the deceased. He didn't have any ID, and his prints didn't show up in our database, and I need to know if you recognize him."

She took the phone and peered at the screen. Matt waited for a reaction of any kind, but she simply stared at the photo. "This man is really dead?"

"Yes. Gunshot wound to the chest."

"I don't know him." She passed the phone back to Matt and sat peering over his shoulder. "Does he have a connection to Grady?"

Matt shared his conversation with Zeke with her.

She locked gazes with him. "You think Grady killed this guy, right?"

"Yes, but I have no proof of that."

The rosy color drained from her cheeks, and her gaze darted around the space before she jumped to her feet and started pacing. "If he committed murder once, it's only a matter of time before he kills me."

Matt had thought the same thing, and nothing had changed his mind. But that was as far as it would go. He wouldn't share his opinion with Nicole and make things harder for her. In fact, he would do his best to ease her mind.

He stood and stepped in her path to stop her. She halted a few feet away, and he had to admit he was tempted to draw her into his arms again. Seemed as if she belonged there. But he'd just recommitted to giving his all to his work and holding her could be leading her on when he had no intention of following through.

He shoved his hands in his pockets and focused on the positives. "Zeke could be wrong. Eyewitnesses often are, and we have no proof that the victim was involved with Harmon."

She nodded as if buying his explanation, but her hands still trembled. "So what happens now?"

"The ME is doing the autopsy. I'll head over there to retrieve the slug. We'll compare it to the one fired at you and to the motel room discharge."

"If they match, then you'll have a firm connection to Grady."

"Yes."

"And then what?"

"I just received Harmon's historical phone data. I'll review that and hope one of the numbers will lead to John Doe's identity and hopefully that will give us a lead on where to find Harmon."

She nodded but said nothing else.

Matt got it. There was nothing else to say. Not when it was looking like Harmon was a murderer. And as she'd said, he could come for Nicole next. Harmon had nothing to lose now and wouldn't hesitate to kill again.

The afternoon dragged on for Nicole. She felt so alone with Matt attending the autopsy and then working in his father's study on the phone records. She'd really come to not only depend on Matt, but she also liked having him around.

She'd tried to keep busy helping Nana and Winnie prepare for a big dinner with all of Matt's siblings and Braden and Lexie but Nicole's mind kept straying to the murder. When they sat down to the table, her stomach was tied in a knot, and she could barely look at the perfectly roasted beef surrounded by carrots, potatoes and onions or the plump biscuits piled high on a large platter.

Sure, she was glad to meet Gavin and his wife, who simply glowed with happiness. And Tessa's fiancé, Braden, too. He seemed like a stand-up guy. But though Nicole put food on her plate, she just kept moving it around. Emilie, on the other hand, once again sitting on Matt's lap, had gobbled hers up to get to the Christmas cookie dessert.

Nicole loved the way her daughter had blossomed at the McKades' ranch. It had nothing to do with the ranch or the country air, but the love and attention of the McKade family. Maybe once Grady was behind bars, Nicole really should move back to Minnesota, allowing Emilie to spend more time with her grandparents and cousins.

She couldn't do that unless Grady was arrested, and that wouldn't happen if she didn't stay in town, allowing Matt to locate Grady. She still wanted to run, to take off and not look back, but she now knew she had to give that up and stay here for the duration. Otherwise, she'd be sealing her and Emilie's future. They'd live a life on the run, always looking for Grady in the rearview mirror, and that would be horrible for both of them.

Gavin cleared his voice, drawing her attention and that of other family members.

"We have an announcement that Lexie is busting a gut to say." Gavin slid his arm around his wife and smiled at her. Love beamed from his face.

Nicole felt an overwhelming desire to have a man look at her that way. Not that she needed someone in her life, but she missed the companionship and joy she'd once had in her marriage with Troy.

Lexie tucked a strand of blond hair behind her ear, and her bright blue eyes twinkled with delight. A broad smile found her face and she peered up at her husband. "We're expecting."

"You're pregnant?" Winnie's voice erupted.

Lexie nodded vigorously. Applause, smiles and shouts of joy traveled around the table.

"I'm going to be a grandmother." Winnie raced around the table to Lexie and drew her into her arms. "When, sweetheart?"

"June."

"Well, I'll be." Walt beamed with happiness and pumped his son's hand.

Betty was soon on her feet and hugging Gavin. "And I'm going to be a great-grandmother. Oh, my. Oh, my." She fanned her face. "I can't wait to have a child in the house again."

"But I'm here," Emilie said, her eyes a mass of confusion.

Nicole held her breath and waited for her daughter to cry.

Betty turned to pat Emilie's cheek and smiled at her

with such love that Nicole had to bite her lip not to gasp. "And I'm enjoying every minute with you, precious."

Emilie beamed up at Betty. "Can we have cookies now?"

Nicole was mortified at her daughter's lack of manners, but laughter rang around the table and she found herself smiling along with the family.

"Of course you can, sweetheart. I'll get them." Betty bent to kiss the top of Emilie's head. "You're a very special young lady."

"I know," Emilie said, earning another round of laughter. She looked confused by the laughter, and her chin trembled.

Matt turned her to face him. "Promise you'll share at least one cookie with me."

She looked up at him and smiled. "You can have a star. They're little. I want the big ones."

Matt's lips turned up in that boyish smile that tugged at Nicole's heart, and she couldn't look away from the gentle expression in his eyes as he smiled at her daughter. Tears pricked Nicole's eyes. Tears of confusion for her fatherless child, who deserved a big happy family like the McKades and would be heartbroken when they had to say goodbye.

It hit her then. She'd come to trust Matt. To believe he was who he said he was. That he had her and Emilie's best interest at heart. After all, hadn't he demonstrated that time and time again? Her heart blossomed, and her mind traveled to future possibilities.

Could she have a future with him?

His phone rang, and his smile evaporated. He dug it out of his pocket.

"Sorry, it's work," he said and answered.

"Always something." Winnie shook her head and scowled.

Nicole was surprised to see her frustration. She hadn't expressed even a peep of being disillusioned about having a family in law enforcement until this very moment.

Was this what Nicole would have to look forward to if she ever got together with Matt? Likely, but she thought she could handle it. Her bubble burst. It didn't matter whether or not she could manage it. He'd made it perfectly clear that he wasn't interested in a relationship. His job came first. And that meant not only before Nicole but before Emilie. Nicole wouldn't put her child through something like that.

"You're positive?" Matt listened intently, and Nicole wished she could hear what the caller was saying.

He said a quick thank-you and goodbye before bending over Emilie. "Hey, little bit. Can you go help Nana get the cookies?"

"Sure." She wiggled down and ran into the kitchen.

Matt turned his attention to Nicole, and at the renewed unease in his expression, her heart dropped. "What is it?"

"We have the ballistics information on the slug from John Doe."

"And?" she asked but could hardly breathe as she waited for his response.

"The rifling matches the slug from the motel room and the shooting outside the garage."

"Then it's official. Grady killed this man. And he was likely trying to kill me outside the garage, too." She wrapped her arms around her stomach and met Matt's gaze. "Please tell me you can stop him before he tries again."

THIRTEEN

"I got this, and you." Matt kept his gaze on Nicole, trying to convince her of his abilities. He wished his whole family wasn't sitting around the table, their gazes darting between the two of them, questions registering in their eyes the longer they stared.

What he wanted was to be alone with Nicole to hold her tight and assure her again that he would keep her safe.

"I need some fresh air." She jumped to her feet. "Would someone mind watching Emilie?"

"Don't worry," his mom said. "We'll keep an eye on her."

Nicole bolted from the room.

Matt didn't let a beat of his heart pass before he ran after her. She was already shrugging into her jacket. "Hold up. You can't go rushing off by yourself. Not with…" He couldn't add "with Harmon gunning for you."

"I'm coming with you."

"You're not planning to try to stop me?"

"I can't imagine Harmon would come here with so many officers in the house, but we'll take Echo with us just in case. If there's any danger, she'll alert us to the problem long before we notice anything."

He got permission from Tessa for Echo to come along,

then put on her leash and grabbed his jacket. Nicole was still trying to get her coat zipped, but her hands trembled badly, and she couldn't pull the tab up.

Matt took over for her and tugged it up to the top. "Ready?"

She nodded, but he saw tears welling in her eyes.

He resisted taking her into his arms. No way was he giving his nosy family something to gossip about while they were gone. He picked up Echo's leash and opened the door before they stepped into the beautiful but very cold night. Stars sparkled above, and Christmas lights twinkled along the garland on the railing. He wished they were years in the future, when he'd been elected sheriff and had figured out the job, and they'd gotten married.

But suddenly he saw Emilie as an older child. Maybe eight or nine. And he would've missed out on all those years in between. He wanted to see her grow up. Be there when she skinned her knees and kiss away her pain. Teach her how to ride a horse and maybe enroll her in Tessa's barrel riding clinic. He wanted that and much more.

A pain knifed into his chest, and he could hardly breathe. He came to a stop, staring out over the ranch. Over Nicole.

She turned to look at him. "Are you coming?"

He nodded, but still couldn't move.

"Is something else wrong? Something you're not telling me?"

Her probing questions brought him back to his senses, and he stowed his thoughts to jog down the stairs. "Let's check on the cabins for the night. Then Granddad won't have to come out in the cold."

She blew on her hands for warmth and started off. "Seems like a year since you found us in the cabin."

"I know. It feels like I've known you for a long time."

"I feel the same way."

He reached out for her hand, and she didn't protest. They walked in silence, the brisk wind keeping Matt moving faster than he'd like, as that meant their walk would end sooner. Echo trotted along next to them. They reached the cabins, and he checked the first five, but when they reached the one where he'd found Nicole the other night, he felt her start shaking. He looked at her, and those tears he'd seen at the house were now running down her cheeks.

"Hey." He stopped and urged her to look up at him. "Don't cry."

"I'm sorry, but I… This is all too much."

He released her hand and gently wiped her tears. "Everything will be okay."

"When you say that, I actually believe it. For a little while. Then something else happens, and I lose it."

"That's the way investigations go. Our progress is rarely straightforward. More like a zigzag."

She leaned into his hand. "I'm so thankful for your care. For your family's care."

"It's no biggie."

"But it is. You don't even see how special your family is." She took a shuddering breath. "It's through them, you, that I now know there are still good men in this world."

Matt's spirits lifted with her praise. She saw him now. The man he tried to be. And she could trust him. He slid his arms around her waist and drew her closer. He'd already kissed her once, and the memory was so heady that he couldn't stop himself again. He lowered his head and met her lips, cold from the night air. She readily responded, but he knew in his heart that it was wrong to lead her on this way.

He forced himself to lift his head and stand back. "I have all these feelings for you, and I don't know what to do with them."

"I understand, I..." She shrugged.

"I still need to think about the election. I've made this commitment to my town and my family to run for sheriff, and I can't just ignore that, but I want—"

Echo growled and pulled on the leash, straining to pull Matt around the side of the cabin. There was no doubt that the dog desperately wanted to check something out.

"What do you think it is?" Nicole clutched Matt's arm.

"Could just be a rodent or animal."

"Help!" a male voice cried out.

"Grady." Nicole spun.

Harmon, here?

Matt pushed Nicole behind his body and drew his weapon, then moved them to the cabin wall and out of Harmon's firing range. Matt poked his head around the corner and scanned the darkness but couldn't see anything. "If you're out there, Harmon, come out with your hands on your head."

"Can't," the man said, his voice weak. "Been shot."

Matt's worry increased tenfold, and he raised his gun. "Is the shooter here?"

"No."

Matt couldn't take the word of a potential killer. He moved Nicole toward the cabin door. He unlocked it, let her in, and grabbed the flashlight they kept under the kitchen cupboard for their guests.

"Go into the bathroom where there're no windows." Matt turned on the flashlight to make sure it worked. "I'll check on him."

"But I—"

Matt clicked off the flashlight. "No buts. I need to know you're safe, so I'm not distracted."

"Then I'll stay put."

He waited for her to cross the room and enter the bathroom. Once she'd closed and secured the door, he locked the front door, too. He circled the structure to approach Harmon from the back. Matt could only hope Harmon wasn't trying to pull something by drawing him away from Nicole.

Matt shot a look around the final corner. He spotted a man of Harmon's size leaning against the wall with one arm. Matt lifted his gun and started his approach. He was just about to call out to the man to put his hands on his head when he crumpled to the ground.

"Harmon!" Matt called out.

He didn't respond and lay unmoving. Matt slowly eased closer. He turned on the flashlight and held it next to his gun out and ready until he reached the man.

"Harmon," he said again, but the man didn't respond.

Fearing a trap, Matt shone the light on the guy's face to confirm his identity, then ran it down the man's body. His hands rested against his stomach, blood oozing between his fingers.

Matt ran the light over the area to be sure they were alone. Satisfied he wasn't in danger, he holstered his weapon and shrugged out of his jacket. He squatted by Harmon to press the fabric on the wound and stem the bleeding.

Harmon moaned in pain. "Nicole. I have to…"

"Have to what?" Matt asked.

Harmon's only response was labored breathing. Matt held the jacket with one hand and dialed 911 to request an ambulance with the other. He wanted to go inside to tell Nicole that she was safe, but he couldn't release his hand or Harmon might bleed out. Matt respected all life, even the life of a killer.

He speed-dialed Kendall and perched the phone between his ear and shoulder.

"I've got Harmon," he said when she answered. "We're by cabin six. He's been shot. I already called for an ambulance, but I want you to escort him to the hospital."

"On my way."

Matt stowed his phone and remained with his hands pressing against Harmon's abdomen. Before long, he heard running footfalls heading his way. He looked up to see Kendall and his dad making their way toward him.

"Nicole's locked in the bathroom," Matt said. "Can one of you tell her about Harmon and that it's safe to come out?"

"Nicole," Harmon said on a breath.

"I'll tell her," Kendall replied.

Matt was thankful she'd offered as she would break the news more gently to Nicole than his father would.

"Nicole," Harmon whispered again.

"What're you trying to tell her?" Matt asked.

Matt heard hurried footsteps, and his dad's hand went to his weapon as he spun. "You like to scare me to death, Nicole. You'll want to stop right there. No need to take a look."

"I have to." Nicole pushed past his father and stopped to clamp a hand over her mouth.

"Why don't you go back inside, Nicole?" Matt suggested.

"Be careful, Nicole," Harmon whispered louder now, his tone urgent. "It's not me… Premier. It's them. Watch your back."

"What?" Matt said. "Premier? Who or what's premier?"

Harmon didn't respond.

"Harmon, tell us," Matt demanded. "We need to know."

His only response was a moan that mingled with the ambulance's spiraling siren in the distance.

Nicole was back at the McKades' dinner table. Most everyone sat in the same chairs, in the room where Lexie and Gavin had only recently shared their exciting news. Now this?

Nicole could barely fathom all that had happened since then. She looked at the empty chairs where Betty, Tessa and Kendall had sat, and Nicole wished they could all go back a few hours to that joyous dinner. But Betty had taken Emilie up to bed to allow the group to discuss Grady's near-death. Tessa was processing the scene where they'd found Grady, and Kendall had followed the ambulance to the hospital to take his statement if he recovered.

"Who thinks Harmon was trying to warn Nicole or just blowing smoke?" Matt asked and once again Nicole was thankful for his levelheaded thinking. And thankful that he'd cleaned up and changed clothing that had been covered in Grady's blood.

"It would be pretty hard for a guy that far gone to have the wherewithal to lie," Jed said.

Walt sipped on his coffee mug. "I have to agree with Dad on this one."

"Any thoughts on what he meant by 'premier'?" Matt asked.

"It could mean a lot of things, but it sounds like a business name to me," Gavin weighed in.

Nicole was glad to have yet one more experienced officer in her corner. "Could it be the company Grady worked security for?"

"If Kendall was here, she'd tell us to look online," Lexie said.

"She would, wouldn't she?" Matt smiled, showing his fondness for his sister.

Nicole looked around the group. "I don't understand."

"She has a computer forensics degree," Matt explained.

"But she's a deputy."

"With today's digital world, the two go hand in hand."

"And she never lets me forget it," Walt said good-naturedly.

"She's right," Matt said. "And she's used her computer skills many times to help us figure things out."

"That she has," Walt acknowledged.

Matt took out his phone. "Let's assume Premier is a business. I'll look it up to see what I can find."

"I'll do the same thing." Gavin dug out his phone, too.

For some reason, she expected Walt to comment, but he sat at the head of the table looking preoccupied. She suspected he was thinking—perhaps about Kendall or even Grady—and when Walt had something to offer the discussion, he would add it.

Matt looked up. "You seeing as many businesses in Austin named Premier as I am, bro?"

Gavin nodded. "Event management firms, physicians, pool builders, insurance companies. The list is endless."

Matt dropped his phone onto the table. "There's no way to narrow it down."

"There has to be a way, doesn't there?" Winnie asked.

"Maybe you can call Harmon's LT again," Walt suggested.

"He was pretty closemouthed, but it can't hurt to try." Matt picked up his phone again and tapped the screen. He was soon recounting details of the shooting before falling silent and drumming his fingers on the table. "Come on, Ackerman. Harmon's been shot. Isn't it time you cooperate so we can figure out who did this?"

Matt listened intently, a frown developing and deepening as he did. "Then get permission and do it fast." Matt shook his head and put his phone on the table. "The guy at least agreed to run it up the flagpole to see if he can get permission to share the employer's name."

The front door opened, and Tessa stepped into the room. She was wearing a white coverall bunched up around her waist, and she had plastic glasses on her forehead. Her knees were covered in grass stains mixed with dried blood.

"Ah, honey, you never looked so irresistible," Braden teased as he got up to cross over to her.

She mocked a flirty pose and grinned at him. He bent down to kiss her cheek, the simple gesture making Tessa's face color nearly as red as her fiery hair.

"You need something, Tessa?" Matt asked.

"We searched Harmon before the medics took him away," Tessa said. "And we recovered his gun."

"And?" Matt and his father asked at the same time, looking so alike that Nicole knew that was what Matt would look like in thirty years. Walt was still fit, handsome and strong, like his son. Not bad genes for Matt to inherit, and she had to admit she wanted to be around to see him then.

"Harmon was carrying a Sig and couldn't have fired any of the slugs we recovered."

Nicole's chin about hit the table. "Grady didn't shoot at me?"

"It's normal for an officer on duty to have a personal backup gun in addition to his service weapon," Gavin said. "He could be carrying two or even more guns."

"Yeah, I thought that, too," Tessa said. "Until I didn't."

"Explain," Walt demanded, his tone sharp.

Tessa cringed, and Braden put a protective arm around her and glared at Walt.

"Sorry," Walt said. "But sometimes you young people take forever to say anything."

Winnie tsked. "You're beginning to sound like a grumpy old man, Walt McKade. Is this the guy I can look forward to having around the house when you retire?"

"Of course not." He blew out such a long breath Nicole thought he might deflate. "My apologies to everyone. Go ahead, Tessa."

"I just heard from the deputies who were combing the area looking for the rental car."

"And they found it?" Matt asked.

Tessa nodded. "The Escalade held all of Harmon's possessions, but no additional guns."

"Okay, let's say Harmon murdered John Doe," Matt said. "It would make sense that he got rid of that gun."

"True that," Braden said, his arm still around his wife, but his humorous expression was long gone. "The missing key here is John Doe's ID. Figure that out, and you'll likely understand how this all relates to Nicole."

"If it even *is* related," Matt muttered.

Nicole locked gazes with Matt. "Are you thinking the murder and Grady being shot might not have anything to do with me?"

"It's possible. If Harmon's cryptic message about Premier is true, he could be dealing with something totally unrelated to you. Then when he came here to find you, it followed him."

Nicole couldn't even believe this news. Why would Grady follow her there if someone was after him? And how would that explain the knife in her apartment? It wouldn't but she had one more question that was more pressing. "But why did someone shoot at me, then?"

Matt shrugged and shoved his hand in his hair. "All I know right now is we need to catch a break soon."

Or else, she heard in his voice, but he didn't say it aloud.

Or else the shooter might come looking for her again.

FOURTEEN

Matt waited by his computer in his dad's office, hoping any minute to get an approved search warrant for Harmon's apartment. He refreshed his inbox again. He opened an email to see a warrant attached.

"Yes!" He sent it to the printer.

Even though Harmon had been shot and had violated a restraining order when he showed up at the ranch, the law still protected his privacy. Meaning Matt still needed a warrant to access the place.

He snatched the paper from the printer and folded it to shove into his jacket pocket. It felt great to finally be moving forward. But before he went in search of Nicole to tell her he was off to Austin, he dialed Harmon's supervisor again. The lieutenant hadn't called back about the company Harmon worked for and their internet search was a bust.

The phone rang five times and the call went to voice mail. Matt left an urgent message. All of this could be over if Harmon would just wake up and answer their questions. He was out of surgery, and it looked like he would recover. He was in and out of consciousness, but the doctor wouldn't let Kendall interview him yet. She would the moment she got the go-ahead from the doctors. Meanwhile, the firearms expert was processing the slug removed from Harmon's chest, and hopefully that would give Matt something to go on.

He headed down the hallway and found Nicole in the foyer, fingering Emilie's ornament on the big tree. He joined her, and the sight of the many familiar ornaments tugged at Matt's already raw emotions. He could honestly say that he would like to see a trio of snowmen on their tree. Two big ones connected together for him and Nicole and this smaller one for Emilie. Or maybe a family of snowmen like his parents had, one he'd always imagined would be on that tree for him someday.

Exactly when had he decided to put marriage and family aside in favor of work? He'd never seen his dad or granddad do that for long. Sure, they both worked long hours, but they usually found time for dinner around the big table. For vacations. To come to his school events. Football games. Teach him how to shoot, hunt and ride.

And they were both great sheriffs.

Did he think he was less of a man than them? Less able?

He just didn't know. It was simply there in his heart and mind. He sighed.

Nicole must have heard him, and she turned to look at him, the ornament in her hand. "Who made this?"

"Nana. She makes one for each family member." He pointed at the recent addition of Braden's ornament.

Nicole turned to look at it. "When are they getting married?"

"In the spring."

She looked back at him. "They seem very happy."

Matt nodded, but his thoughts went to Tessa and Braden having worked through many issues to get to the point where they were now. Gavin and Lexie, too.

Was Matt going through the same thing with Nicole? Was there hope for them?

Anything was possible, he supposed, but *nothing* was possible if Harmon's shooter got to Nicole before Matt could figure things out. He needed to get moving on that. "I received a warrant to search Harmon's apartment, and I'm heading to Austin now. Dad and Granddad will be here for—"

"I'm going with you."

He opened his mouth to argue.

She quickly flashed up her hand. "I know Grady better than you do and can answer any questions you might have about what you find at his place."

With Harmon in custody, albeit in a hospital bed, he couldn't harm her, but what if his shooter really was gunning for Nicole? Wasn't it safer for her to hang out at the ranch with his father and granddad? "I don't know. I—"

She grabbed his arm. "Grady can't hurt me, and if there *is* another guy in town looking for me, it's dark out now and headlights make it easier to determine if we're followed, right?"

"Right," Matt said and couldn't fault her logic. "But I don't—"

She squeezed his arm and peered into his eyes. "Please. I can't just sit around here. I have to help." She moved closer. "Please."

Those eyes, so blue and wide, were fixed on his, and he had no defenses against what they did to him. "Okay, but you have to listen to my every direction. And I'll want to have an officer clear his place first. Just in case someone is waiting for him to come home."

"Of course I'll listen. I promise." She threw her arms around his neck and hugged him hard. "Thank you. This means a lot to me."

"Let me just tell Dad what's going on and ask Mom to watch Emilie."

"Thank you and thank her," Nicole said.

Matt headed into the family room, where his parents and grandparents were watching *Gunsmoke*. "Change of plans. Nicole is coming with me. She knows Harmon best and might see something I miss or better interpret what I do find."

"You be careful," his mother said. "We'll take care of Emilie, and I'll pray you find what you're looking for."

"Ditto that," his nana added. "And watch out for our sweet Nicole. I like her, Grandson. Really like her."

"Me, too," his mother added. "And don't get us started on adorable little Emilie."

Matt loved how his family had embraced Nicole and Emilie, and he was suddenly choked up as he thought about them leaving his family when she was once again safe. He didn't trust himself to speak and thank them so he just nodded.

Nicole had her jacket on and was slipping into her boots. Since he was going in his official capacity, he'd changed into his uniform, so he grabbed his work jacket from the hallway hook. No way he would breach a man's front door and not be in uniform.

Once they were on the road, he kept checking his mirrors to watch for a tail. He even made a few left turns to be sure no one was following.

"Are we alone?" Nicole asked.

He nodded and suddenly became aware of being just inches away from her. He could easily reach out for her hand. But he wouldn't. Not when he needed to keep watching for any danger.

"You wouldn't happen to have a key to Harmon's apartment, would you?" he asked. "Otherwise, I'll have to find the manager to let me in. This late at night, he won't likely be eager to help out."

"I have a key. At my place. I tried to give it back to Grady, but he refused. He said that would mean we were truly over." She sighed. "I wanted to throw it away, but figured if I did, he'd come back for it and then accuse me of lying to him."

Matt met her gaze. "Have I mentioned how sorry I am that he put you through all of this?"

"Thank you, but as I said before it's my fault. If I'd only listened to God, I would have waited for a Christian man to date."

"Christians do bad things, too, you know."

"I know."

He nodded. "How are you doing on forgiving yourself?"

"I don't know. I mean, I haven't let it go, that's for sure. But I want to now. Which is a step in the right direction. Before, I didn't have hope that I might ever be right with God again."

"And now you do?"

She nodded.

"Mind if I ask how that happened?"

"Your family. You. Your care. Encouragement." She sighed. "Your parents and grandparents remind me of mine. Living their faith. Opening their hearts to people in trouble. They took me and Emilie in without question. And they've been so welcoming. I can never repay them."

"And me?" he asked, hating that he needed to. "When we first met, you compared me to Harmon."

She swiveled to face him. "You're in law enforcement and have some of the same tendencies. That's inevitable."

He hoped there was a "but" coming, but he had enough pride that he couldn't ask that, too.

"But deep down, in here." She touched his chest. "Where it really matters, you're nothing like Grady. I see it every time you hold Emilie. Every time you help me. Pretty much all the time."

He pressed his hand over hers and wanted to linger in the ease between them. But he couldn't. Not now. He had to keep his mind on business, his eyes open. No way would he let someone put her life in danger again.

Nicole had only been gone from her apartment for a few days, but it already smelled stale. There were dirty dishes in the sink, and she wanted to take care of them but finding the man who shot Grady was far more important.

She went straight to her desk in the family room corner and grabbed the key.

"Do you want to get anything else while you're here?" Matt asked.

She looked at Emilie's presents under the tree. Christmas was only two days away.

"You can bring them, if you want," Matt said.

"Do you really think we'll still be at the ranch on Christmas?" she asked, and realized she wished they would be there. Not because Matt hadn't found the shooter and arrested him, but because she could simply choose to stay with the McKades for that special day.

His eyes narrowed, and he clearly didn't like her question. She wanted to reach up and ease out the wrinkle above his nose with her touch, but she refrained from doing so.

"That was a silly question." She laughed it off. "You'll figure this out before then. I know you will."

"It's not that. I…" He let his words fall off.

She wanted to encourage him to continue, but she

also wanted him just to say whatever he had to say of his own accord.

"Even when this is all resolved, I don't want you to leave Lost Creek, but I don't really have anything to offer you." He ran a hand over the dark stubble on his jaw. "My goals for the next few years are mapped out, and I can't change that."

Right. That again. She knew he didn't want a relationship, so why did hearing him say it cut her to the core? Because she'd fallen for him. Big-time. But she wouldn't beg him to be with her and Emilie. Not when he wasn't ready for it. That might be even worse than being with a guy like Grady.

She held up the key. "We should get going, right?"

He nodded but didn't look all that convinced. He gestured for her to precede him, and she took one last look at the tree before starting for the door.

It was suddenly kicked in.

She screamed and lurched back as two men holding rifles burst inside.

Matt grabbed her arm and pushed her behind his body but she got a quick look at the men first. One was tall. One short. Both in dark clothing. Neither wearing masks, revealing mean-looking expressions on faces she'd never seen before.

She couldn't see around Matt and heard the door close.

"Sit," one of the men demanded, his voice deep and gravelly. "On the floor now."

"Hey, come on," Matt said. "There's no need for this. Just tell me what you want, and we can work it out."

Nicole risked a peek around Matt to see the biggest man lifting his weapon and marching toward them. A jarring crunch of bone sounded, and Matt was pushed backward. His hand went up to his head, but he didn't cry out.

"If you don't want me to hit the little woman the same way, I suggest you sit," the guy snapped.

Matt turned to Nicole. Blood streamed from his forehead and through his fingers.

"You're bleeding," she said, wishing she could help this man who had come to mean so much to her, but she held back, knowing the gunman wouldn't like it and might strike Matt again. "I'll get some bandages."

"Sit," the man demanded, his icy stare stopping her in place. "Now. On the floor."

She lowered herself to the carpet, and Matt sat next to her. He kept his hand pressed on his head but took her hand with his free one.

"Isn't that touching?" The tall guy fixed his rifle on them. "Get to it, Roger."

"But, Hal," the guy whined, his voice and posture pegging him as the weaker of the two. "I want to stand guard for once."

"Then get a brain, and maybe I'll let you," Hal laughed.

The less intimidating man dumped a pillowcase on the floor. Rope and bandannas spilled out.

"Now, the two of you put your phones on the floor." Hal gestured at them.

"Mine's already on the counter," Nicole said.

Hal glanced at the kitchen. "Then it's only you, cowboy."

Matt glared at Hal as he dug out his phone and dropped it on the carpet.

"Hands behind your backs," Roger said. "Both of you."

Matt squeezed her hand and let go to place his hands behind his body as requested. She followed suit. Roger tied Matt up first and took his gun.

"Who are you?" Matt asked. "What's this about?"

"Shut up," Hal said. "Or I'll plug your sweetie, here."

She didn't doubt he would do it and refrained from asking any questions of her own. Besides, the way her heart was thundering in her chest and pounding like a bass drum, she figured she wouldn't get out a coherent sentence anyway.

Roger tugged hard on the rope and moved over to her. He wound the rope around her wrists, and the scratchy texture bit her wrists. She wanted to cry out but took a hint from Matt's strength and wouldn't let these men know they were hurting her. Next came a bandanna around her mouth. He pulled it hard, and the cloth immediately dried her mouth She fought back her gag reflex.

Matt looked at her and smiled. He was transmitting his confidence to get them out of this situation, and she tried not to worry, but bad thoughts—horrific thoughts—barreled through her brain.

Were they going to die? Would she ever see Emilie again? Ever hold her, kiss her precious baby? Tears flooded her eyes, and she started choking.

"Look at me, honey." Matt bent forward to make eye contact.

She focused on the familiar planes of his face. His eyes that held such affection for her. The scary thoughts suddenly seemed less terrifying.

"Ain't it touching, Roger?" Hal said and pretended to cry.

"Yeah. Touching." Roger moved behind Matt and slid the bandanna between his lips. Matt never took his eyes from her, and she continued to feel his strength.

"Okay, this is how things are going to go," Hal said. "I'll take the little lady out to my vehicle first. Roger will stay here to guard the cowboy. You try anything, cowboy, and I'll shoot the lady. Both of you nod if you understand."

Matt nodded, and she did, too.

Hal planted a big, meaty hand on her arm and jerked her to her feet. He dragged her to the door, pausing to glance outside, likely to make sure no one saw them. She peered at Matt, and if eyes could smile and say, "Don't worry, everything will be okay," his did.

She nodded, telling him she got his message. She was suddenly jerked out the door, and she could hardly keep up with Hal's long strides. He went to the back of an older-model Ford sedan with rusted sides and inserted a key in the trunk. The lock popped, then he picked her up and dumped her onto the hard floor.

What? She'd thought he was retrieving something. But no, he'd put her inside the trunk. He closed the trunk with a resounding thump. All light vanished. She was bound and gagged in a trunk. Alone.

Her heart nearly pounded through her chest.

What if they simply wanted to abduct her and had no intention of bringing Matt along? Was that talking about bringing him with them just a ruse to make her compliant?

Panic raced through her veins.

She kicked at the lid. Kicked the walls. Anywhere she could lash out, but nothing helped.

She lay back, panting from her exertion. She could hardly breathe with her mouth gagged, so she pulled in slow breaths through her nose, blew them out, all the while thinking of how Matt had looked at her.

Calmer now, she listened. Heard footfalls. Two sets or three, she couldn't tell. She waited for Hal to open the trunk. He didn't. Two car doors opened. Then slammed.

Had he really left Matt in the apartment? Was she all alone?

Oh, God, no. Please, no.

FIFTEEN

The car seemed to travel for hours. Nicole counted to keep her mind busy but kept losing track. The vehicle must have veered off the main road, since it felt like they were rolling over crunchy gravel. Hal didn't slow down, though. The car bumped hard, hitting ruts, and tossing her around like a beanbag in a corn hole game.

Where in the world were they taking her?

God, please, she cried out in her mind. She had no right to be calling out, but she needed Him.

Her faith was weak, and this was too much for her to handle all alone. What kind of Christian did that make her? She became desperate and then she asked for God's help when all these months she'd backed away from Him.

I'm sorry. I should have listened to Matt. You were there all along. Hearing my confession. Forgiving me.

She thought of Emilie and how she wanted to be a big girl at times and didn't want to take Nicole's hand, but Nicole clutched it tightly anyway to keep her daughter safe. God was the same way. Exactly like He'd promised in Isaiah, He'd been reaching out for Nicole's hand, promising to help her and telling her not to fear. But Nicole had let go. Tried to prove what a big girl she was.

Tears pricked her eyes and rolled down her cheeks. She sobbed uncontrollably. For herself. For Emilie. For Matt.

God, I'm sorry. Please don't let my foolishness cause either of them any harm.

Her sinuses filled from crying and breathing became even more difficult. She heard the lyrics from her favorite song in her mind. God was there. No matter what. Her refuge. Her peace in tough times. All she had to do was cling to Him.

If she remembered that, everything would be fine.

The car slowed and turned. Started moving over even rougher ground. She was thrown against the top. The side. Each bump pain-filled. Suddenly the vehicle came to a stop, and she rolled to the front of the trunk.

She heard two doors open and close again. Then nothing. She counted.

One, two, three.

Breathed deep.

Four, five, six.

Kept counting. Hit four hundred and the trunk opened. She searched above. Saw stars glimmering in the sky and tall cypress trees.

Hal jerked her out and settled her on her feet as if she was a rag doll. She got her footing and took a look around. A ramshackle ranch house sat in the distance. It looked like it was habitable only by wildlife, but a light burned bright inside.

Three small outbuildings were off in the distance where an oil pump thumped in a steady rhythm. Why had they brought her to an abandoned ranch that seemed only useful for pulling oil from the ground?

He pushed her ahead, and she searched the car for Matt. Saw no one. She wished she could talk. She'd ask about him or better yet call out for him.

She slowed to get a better look at the place, but Hal shoved her ahead and kept going until they reached a rustic outbuilding. Roger stood by the door, rifle in hand. As he opened the door, she noted a new hasp had been added and a padlock hung open.

They were going to lock her up out here, but why?

Hal gave her another shove. She stumbled inside. Without the overhead light from the moon, the interior was dark and shadowy. She could only imagine the creepy crawlies in this place. A movement ahead startled her, and she jumped back.

Hal laughed. "What's wrong? Afraid of your boyfriend now? He's sitting right here. Waiting for you."

"Matt," surprise had her crying out but it came out sounding nothing like his name.

A similar sound came from Matt, and she decided to believe he'd called out her name. She took baby steps across the small space until she felt his boot. Hal pushed her to the hard ground and laughed as he backed out of the tiny space.

She heard the hasp rasp over the other piece and the padlock snick into place.

"Have fun, you two," Hal said and then his footsteps receded.

Did she hear Roger's, too, or was he still out there?

Were the creepy guys leaving them alone? Here. Out in nowhere. Would they come back for them or let them die here?

She scooted around until she was sitting next to Matt. His knee pressed into hers. She desperately wanted to speak to him. Communicate. Touch him with her hands. But all of that was impossible. His knee pressed tighter.

Yes. He knew she needed to connect with him. Knew

she needed her fears calmed, and his nearness did just that, dispel a bit of her fear.

She lifted her face as if God could see her. Mentally reached out for His hand. All would be well with Him. Maybe what she wanted would happen, maybe not, but whatever God deemed appropriate to happen right now would turn out for their own good.

Even letting myself love Matt would, right, God? He's a believer and a fine man. You put him in my life, didn't You?

The peace that settled into her heart told her all she needed to know. If Matt ever asked her out, dating him wouldn't be a mistake. Everything would be okay. All she needed to do was trust God and leave everything else up to Him.

Nicole rested her head on Matt's shoulder, and he loved the feel of her so close. She was trying to tell him something, and he wanted to think she was showing that she cared for him. Why he thought that, he didn't know, but he did. She wasn't crying or shivering in fear but seemed oddly calm.

Well, he wasn't. They had to get out of this rat hole. These men had let them see their faces and didn't bother to cover Matt's eyes on the drive out there. That meant only one thing. They weren't going to let anyone live. And he had to get free to figure out their location so he could tell someone in his family where to send reinforcements. If only he knew who these guys were and what they wanted, it might help him come up with a plan.

He shifted around, and Nicole lifted her head. He wanted to tell her what he was doing, but he couldn't speak. He got to his feet, made his way to the door and rammed his shoulder into the wood that he hoped would splinter.

"Knock it off," Roger warned from outside. "If I have to come in there, you'll be sorry."

Matt took heed. He'd learned what he needed to know. Roger was still by the door, and hopefully that meant they didn't intend to let them die out here quite yet.

Matt could do nothing else with Roger posted outside as a sentry and made his way back to Nicole. Temperatures had fallen drastically since they'd set out from the ranch, and frigid air seeped through the rotting boards. To warm both of them up, he eased his body close to hers. Her head rested on his shoulder again, and he reveled in the softness of her hair as it brushed against his neck.

If only he was free to kiss her and tell her he wouldn't let anything bad happen to her. But even if he said that, he'd be lying as he couldn't predict what would happen. He wished he could, but only God could save them now.

Father, please, Matt begged. *Please get us out of this mess.*

Matt had to believe there would be an opening for him to act. He would rest as much as he could to be in top form when that time came. He leaned his head back against the splintering wood and stretched his legs out over the dirt floor. He closed his eyes and listened to Nicole's even breathing. Relaxing his muscles, he kept his ears tuned for any sound other than the wind howling through the cracks in the dilapidated building.

Footfalls soon sounded in the distance, big steps pounding urgently over the ground. Nicole's head came up. She'd heard them, too. Was it Hal coming back or someone else?

Matt sat forward and pulled up his knees, readying

himself to fall on Nicole to save her from a gunshot or knife.

A sliver of light filtered under the door and something rustled outside. Matt sat forward, his body tensing. The lock squeaked as the door swung open. A man stood on the threshold, the moonlight haloing his frame and shading his face. He swung up a large lantern and shone it inside.

Matt's eyes balked at the brightness, and he blinked hard. Nicole turned away. Matt blinked again, his eyes continuing to fight the sharp beams as the man swung his lantern.

Matt's eyes finally adjusted, and he ran his gaze over the man who wasn't Hal or Roger. He was tall, maybe six-five, and thin. Like a string bean. He had to bend to step into the shed and was dressed in an expensive tweed coat, dress slacks and shoes. His face was long and pockmarked. And he, like Hal and Roger, evidently didn't care if Matt saw it clearly.

A very bad sign.

He set down the lantern and moved toward Nicole. Matt shoved his body forward, trying to block the guy from touching her.

"Don't worry, I'm just removing your gags so we can talk." His voice was smooth and level, not at all flustered.

He released Nicole's gag and then Matt's.

"Who are you and why have you taken us hostage?" Matt asked, his voice raspy from dryness.

"Stephen Fairhurst. And you can thank Grady Harmon for your present situation."

"Explain," Matt demanded.

Stephen's eyebrows rose, but unlike the thugs who'd grabbed them, he didn't seem a violent type of man.

"Harmon started working as a security guard for our

investment firm about a year ago," he said calmly. "He recently overheard a private conversation and figured out we were laundering money."

"Your firm's name?" Matt asked.

"Premier Investments of Texas."

"Grady warned us about you," Nicole said.

"Of course he did. He's in love with you." Fairhurst smiled. "And here you are with another man." He tsked but it evaporated into a chuckle.

Matt needed to keep him on target and gain as much information as possible. "If you're laundering money, why in the world would you hire a police officer for security?"

"No offense, Deputy, but I've found that most law enforcement officers aren't that bright, and honestly, not overly motivated. Give them a door to guard and they'll stand there, doing nothing else, just like they're told."

Matt lifted his chin. "I'm offended, all right, and you're wrong. You've just run into the wrong officers. Except for Harmon, apparently."

"You're right. Harmon was an exception. It was the oddest thing." He chuckled. "We thought we would have a problem with him when he figured things out, but he surprised us all. He wanted in on the action."

"And you trusted a cop?" Matt asked.

"Enough to have him do a few small jobs that couldn't lead back to us and still give him a chance to prove himself. He was quite good at everything we asked him to do." Fairhurst frowned and stroked his chin with his free hand. "Until he met Nicole."

Matt hated this man even saying her name, and he wished he was free to rip him limb from limb.

"Then Harmon changed. He wanted to do more. Said he needed more money. Wanted to give her the high life like her husband had." Fairhurst shook his head. "Poor Harmon. So insecure. He had to prove he was a bigger man than her dead husband."

"And you took advantage of that," Matt said, disgusted.

"Hey, now." Fairhurst's chin went up at a sharp angle. "The guy wanted in, and he'd proven himself. We only did what he wanted and moved him up to be a liaison for one of our especially difficult clients who is a royal pain. We didn't want to lose him, but we were tired of trying to satisfy him. So we gave Grady a go at it. He was wildly successful at the job and soon became invaluable to us. And then..." Fairhurst sighed and focused on Nicole.

"Then he suddenly wanted out. He never said why, just that we had to part ways. Of course, we couldn't do that. He knew too much. We'd kill him before letting him quit."

"Yeah," Matt said. "I got the impression from your goons who took us that you'd be glad to end the life of anyone who gets in the way."

"But you complied, didn't you? Good decision. Obviously, Harmon isn't as sharp as you and didn't know to heed our warnings." Fairhurst's eyes narrowed, and Matt suddenly got a feel for how dangerous this man really was. "He started ignoring his responsibilities at the firm. We figured he was testing us. Trying to see if we meant business and if we would end his life."

"And you did mean business," Matt said. "I can tell that from your demeanor."

"But..." Fairhurst sighed. "But we still didn't want to have to deal with that pesky client and decided to cut Harmon some slack. Work on keeping him in line."

Matt could just imagine their actions, but he wanted to hear Fairhurst explain. "How'd you do that?"

"The best way possible." A snide grin narrowed already thin lips. "Threaten the woman he desperately loves."

"Me?" Nicole's voice squeaked high.

"Of course, my dear. You got our texts, did you not? The ones with the threats."

"That was you."

"Yes. Who did you think it was?"

"Grady."

"But why?" Fairhurst's eyebrows went up. "Why would he threaten you?"

"He was possessive and controlling, so I broke up with him."

"You did?" Fairhurst's eyes turned angry. "No wonder the threats didn't bring him into line."

"So you didn't know about the restraining order she filed on Harmon?" Matt asked.

"Unfortunately, my people missed that." His look turned deadly serious. "Someone will pay for that screwup."

"I don't understand," Nicole said. "How did you think threatening me would keep Grady in line?"

"We assumed you'd tell Grady about the calls. He'd know it was us and realize if he didn't toe the line that we could get to you."

"The knife on my counter? It was you?" Nicole's voice went higher, and Matt could tell she was close to losing it.

A slow smile spread across Fairhurst's face. "But it turns out Harmon was in the parking lot watching you."

"He stalked me after we broke up."

"My men saw you take off, and Harmon immediately entered your apartment. He must have seen the knife, figured things out and took off. We thought he'd follow you, but he didn't. Instead, he took my men on a wild-goose chase."

"He put a GPS tracker on her car," Matt said.

"He must have been worried you'd hurt me and led you away from me." Nicole shook her head. "I can't believe it. He was protecting me the last few days, not trying to hurt me."

"I have to say, it's hysterical that you thought he was the one trying to hurt you."

"You shot at me?"

"One of my men, yes. After he located Harmon, and he refused to come back, our guy took a potshot at you, figuring it would make Harmon relent."

"How did you even find him?" Nicole asked.

"Harmon isn't the only one who can use a tracker," he laughed. "We sent one of our men after Harmon, but they got into a fight at the motel, and later, Harmon killed our man."

That explained John Doe, but not why she and Matt were captives.

"Why are we here?" Matt asked.

"Bait. It looks like Harmon will recover, and we want him to come looking for Nicole." He grinned. "We weren't quite ready for you, but then you both showed up at the apartment without backup, and we couldn't miss the chance to take you now."

"There's no way you'll get past our guard at the hospital to get word to Harmon. No point in trying," Matt said, suddenly afraid for Kendall's life along with theirs, as Kendall was guarding Harmon.

A self-satisfied look settled on Fairhurst's face. "Let me worry about that. Now sit tight, and once we have Harmon in custody, I'll come back to let you go."

Right. Like that would happen.

"Water," Matt called out to stop Fairhurst. "We need water."

"Of course." He turned to the door. "Roger, bring them some water."

He stepped aside to let in Roger, who twisted the top from a disposable water bottle and poured some into Nicole's mouth first, then Matt's. After a quick drink, he said, "Give the rest to Nicole."

"Now we'll be going," Fairhurst said. "After you, Roger."

Roger scuttled out of the building, and Fairhurst followed, taking the lantern with him and plunging them back into the black of night.

SIXTEEN

A chill settled into Nicole's body. She suspected the temperatures had dropped below freezing in the last hour, but it wasn't just the physical cold that was causing her to shake. She was terrified for her life. For Matt's life.

"Hey," he said, his tone so soft and filled with affection that tears formed in her eyes. "I'll get us out of this. I have a plan."

"But how?" She turned to look at him, though she couldn't even make out his shadow. "They have guns. You have nothing."

"True, but Roger doesn't seem to be the brightest guy, and I can surely outthink him."

"What about Hal? Or Fairhurst? They seem smarter."

"They're not here right now. All I have to do is overpower Roger and get his gun."

"But how? You're tied up."

"Let me worry about that."

He sounded extremely confident, but she couldn't imagine how he could pull this off, and her shaking increased. "I'm afraid, Matt. If anything happened to you, I..."

"Hey, hey," he said soothingly. "I wouldn't try anything if I didn't think I could succeed. Besides, we have to do something. They let us see their faces, and Fairhurst gave us his name. Means he doesn't plan to let us go."

"What? No…no. I didn't think of that." Her mind raced, trying to figure out what he intended to do, and if she could help, but she couldn't think of a way out of this. "Can I help you?"

"Stay right where you are," he replied quickly. "And no matter what happens, don't try to interfere."

"But you'll let me know if you need me?"

"Yes," he said and scooted closer. "I'm going to kiss you now, if that's okay."

"Please," she said and faced him.

His lips sought hers in the dark, missing once, then settling into place over hers. She wished she could twine her arms around his neck and draw him even closer, but with bound hands that was impossible. She settled for leaning even closer and never letting her lips break contact.

Much too soon, he lifted his head. "I could kiss you all night. Honestly, for longer than that." His tone was lighter. "But I have to get moving."

"Wait, don't go. Please. I don't want to lose you." She couldn't believe the desperation in her own voice.

"You won't, honey. I promise." He pressed another kiss against her lips, and she heard him get up and move away.

Noises came from the far corner of the room. She'd searched the space after her eyes had adjusted to the light and remembered seeing a ratty old workbench strewn with trash in that corner, but she was sure there hadn't been any tools for Matt to use to free himself.

"What are you doing?" she whispered loudly.

"Shh," he replied in a hushed tone. "Let's not give Roger a reason to come in here."

She wanted to keep talking. To keep asking, but she had to respect Matt's wishes.

"Unh," he grunted and blew out a long breath.

"Are you okay?" she called out before thinking of Roger.

"Fine," he replied, his tone quiet and strained as if he was in pain. He'd hurt himself. She was certain of that, but he would go on, doing his best to save their lives. She was certain of that as well.

Matt held his breath and counted until the pain subsided. When Fairhurst had been in the shack, Matt had spotted an old tin can sitting in the corner, the lid still attached. Looked like it had been there since people stopped making cans out of tin. He'd tried to saw off his ropes with the top and sliced into his arm, crying out and dropping the can in the process.

He'd should have had the forethought not to cry out, allowing Nicole to hear him. Now she wanted to know what he was up to, but he couldn't very well announce his movements for Roger to overhear. Matt probably should have shared his plans before he started, but he didn't want her to get her hopes up in case he failed.

He'd tried to sound confident for her sake, but he knew things could go wrong. She was already worried for him, and he didn't want to make it worse.

He closed his eyes and concentrated on finding the can as he inched across the floor. His fingers touched the metal.

Yes! He ran them over the tin until he could grasp the open lid. He took a good hold on it, but as he got it moving against the rope, blood ran down the can, making it harder to grasp.

He gritted his teeth and sawed back and forth. Slower this time, in shorter strokes. He heard movement outside.

Was Roger coming to the door?

No. Not now.

He was almost free. He started his hands moving faster. Not caring when the sharp edge nicked his skin. He had to hurry.

He stretched the rope taut. Faster. Faster. Faster, he sawed.

It suddenly broke and dropped away.

Yes! He was free.

He listened for Roger. For any movement. Silence. *Perfect.*

Keeping hold of the can, he jerked his hands around to the front. His muscles screamed from his arms being tied back, but he didn't care. He scooted across the room, can in hand in case he couldn't untie Nicole's rope, then put it by her foot so he could find it again in the dark.

He raised his hands to Nicole's face. Cupped it gently.

"You're free," she cried out.

"Shh." He shouldn't have startled her like that.

"Sorry," she whispered.

"I'm going to work on your ropes now." He felt along her arm until he reached the knot. He dug his fingers in and pulled.

"You're bleeding. I can feel it."

"It's just a scratch."

"No, it's not. Use the bandanna. Tie it off."

"After I finish with the ropes." He kept at the knot until he'd loosened it and freed her. He wanted to shout his thanks to God, but he still had work to do, and they weren't out of danger yet. All manner of things could happen.

First, he needed to listen to Nicole and stop his bleeding. He felt for the cloth and covered his wound. "I got the bandanna wrapped around, but I need you to tie it off."

"Okay." Her fingers landed on his shoulder and crept down his arm to pick up the ends of the bandanna. "This is going to hurt."

"Go ahead." He drew in deep breath and held it.

She tugged the fabric tight. Pain raced up his arm. He bit down on his lip not to cry out. He saw stars and not the good kind. Maybe the cut was worse than he'd thought. He took a few long breaths.

"Okay, now," he said when the pain receded a bit. "I'll move over to the door. You call out to Roger. Tell him you have to go to the bathroom. Keep bugging him until he opens the door. Can you do that?"

"Nag the man who tied me up. You know I can." She chuckled quietly.

Matt was thankful for her sudden good mood. "Kiss me."

She felt for his face and pressed her lips against his. They were cold and delicious and warm all at the same time. He kissed her deeply before pulling back. "Okay, ready to nag?"

"Ready," she said. "As I doubt you'll ever encourage me to nag again."

He stifled a laugh and scooted across the room. He located a board leaning against the wall that he'd seen in the lantern light. He gripped the splintered wood.

"Okay. Stay right where you are so Roger will focus on you and call out to him." Matt lifted the board over his head and waited for the man to open the door.

SEVENTEEN

"Roger!" Nicole shouted. "I have to use the restroom."

"Tough," he replied.

"Stephen won't like it if you don't let me go." She tried to sound convincing, when she knew Stephen couldn't care less if she had the use of a restroom.

"I don't know." His voice wavered.

"He told us as much," she said. "Not about using the restroom, but about asking you for anything we needed. Remember how he had you give us some water? That was because we asked."

"Okay, fine," he snapped.

Before long the hasp moved on the other side of the door. Nicole's heart sang at having succeeded in getting Roger to do her bidding.

The door soon opened. A shaft of moonlight revealed Matt standing tall, a large board in his hands. Roger crossed the threshold. Matt remained locked in place until Roger moved completely inside. She heard him breathe in, and then he swung the board hard.

Roger went down with a solid thud. Matt was on him and jerking his hands behind his back faster than Nicole thought possible.

Matt looked up. "Bring me your rope and gag."

She located them and crawled toward Matt. He quickly tied and gagged Roger.

"Can you help me move him over by the workbench?" Matt asked. "I'll tie him to it and stop him from squirming around and making noise."

She took one arm, Matt the other, and they dragged the man to the corner. Matt tied him to the bench and turned to sweep her into his arms. She almost gasped at the love burning from his eyes. Had he fallen for her, too, and did that mean there really was a future for them?

She wanted to ask, but now wasn't the time to discuss it.

He gave her a kiss, more of a quick peck than anything, and released her. He bent down to Roger and searched his pockets. Matt came up holding a phone, tapped out a number and lifted the cell to his ear. "Dad, it's Matt."

"Where are you, son?" She heard his dad's concerned voice filter through the phone.

Matt described their location and they gave the names of their abductors. She couldn't believe their abductors hadn't blindfolded him, either, but they must have been so confident in their abilities that they'd gotten sloppy. Or maybe they weren't smart enough to think of what they were revealing when they hadn't covered their faces.

"We're headed up to the house now. If I find Fairhurst and his other goon there, I won't confront them. Not with Nicole with me. I'll stake out the house and keep you updated. I wish we were in our jurisdiction, and you could respond, but I'll need you to coordinate with the Travis County Sheriff. I suggest they come in silent to keep from spooking the men. I'll put this phone on vibrate. You can give the sheriff this number, and he can coordinate with me."

Matt listened, but Nicole couldn't hear Walt's response.

"Copy that," Matt said, and she saw him change the phone's settings before shoving it into his pocket. "We should have deputies here soon."

He squatted by the door and came up holding Roger's rifle. He looked ferocious with the moonlight shadowing his face and accentuating his chiseled features.

"C'mon," he said. "Let's get moving. Stay behind me. Grab onto my belt. I want to know you're with me, but I need to keep my entire focus on what's ahead of us."

"Of course," she said. She wasn't about to do anything that would jeopardize her life or the life of the man she now knew she loved.

Matt had told Nicole that the deputies would arrive soon, but Travis County covered a large area, and depending on where the deputies were located at the moment, meant anywhere from a five to fifteen-minute wait.

Until then, Matt had to make sure the other men didn't take off.

He poked his head out of the shed and scanned the area. What he wouldn't give for night vision binoculars and an NVG scope on the rifle, but he'd have to make do with the naked eye. He remembered seeing a line of trees to his right, likely planted as a windbreak for the buildings. Thankfully, the moon had taken cover under a patch of clouds, hiding them as they made their move toward the trees for cover. Unfortunately, it would mean he'd have a harder time navigating and moving ahead would be slow going.

He lifted the rifle and started out. Nicole grabbed his belt and held firm. He squinted, trying to bring the area ahead into focus and avoid any pitfalls. He inched forward. One step. Then another, feeling for secure footing before planting his foot. An owl hooted in the distance. If Matt headed that direction, he'd soon reach the tree line.

He kept going. Slowly. Scanning the area. His heart pounding.

The trees came into view. *Perfect.* He eased ahead and took cover behind a large cypress. He blew a breath before turning to Nicole.

"You doing okay?" He tried to sound like he had it all together when adrenaline was racing through his body and wreaking havoc.

"Fine."

She sounded shaky, but her hand still fixed on his belt wasn't trembling, telling him they were good to move to the next tree. He started off, faster this time. Paused behind the trunk. Scanned the area. They kept going, one tree, then the next. Until the house came into view. A light still burned inside, flowing from the windows and illuminating the immediate area.

He stepped ahead, easing down the windbreak. Movement in a window stopped him cold. He squinted and saw Hal stride past the glass.

Nicole gasped.

Matt glanced back at her. "It's okay. I'm armed, and he won't hurt us."

She nodded, but she didn't seem convinced. He was trained on such maneuvers, but she was a civilian and must be terrified.

"You're doing great," he whispered. "This will soon be over."

He continued to watch until he saw Fairhurst step up to Hal. Matt set down the rifle and dialed his father to give a quick update.

"Deputies are still five minutes out," his dad said.

"Copy that," Matt replied. "We're approaching the house. This will be my last communication with you until we have them in custody."

"Be safe, son. I love you."

His father's declaration took him by surprise, but his dad knew this could still go sideways. "Love you, too, Dad."

Matt shoved the phone in his pocket and picked up the rifle. "We have to move closer. I need a better shot at the front door in case they bolt. We have to be completely silent from here on out."

"I can do that," she said, and he was glad to hear confidence in her tone.

He set off again. Slowly. Methodically, he stepped, willing his feet not to make even a fraction of a sound. He kept going until he had a perfect view of the door.

He turned to Nicole and moved her behind the tree, signaling for her to stay put. She reached out to him. Squeezed his hand. He smiled, but with the moon in hiding, he had no idea if she saw it. He'd kiss her, but he had to keep his focus on the house.

He watched. Time ticked by. One minute. Two. Three.

The outside light snapped on, and the door opened. Hal poked his head out. Matt raised the rifle. Took aim.

A large dog bounded down the steps. Moved to a shrub and lifted its leg.

Matt held his breath. If the dog caught their scent and started barking, it was all over.

No. No. No.

Nicole kept her eyes on the dog, but clutched Matt's shoulder. She could hardly breathe for fear the animal would suddenly sense them, bare his teeth and come running. It was a big dog. Looked like a German shepherd from this distance. Her uncle had one, and he weighed over seventy-five pounds. There was no way they could survive if that animal came for them, short of Matt shooting it, and she doubted he would willingly kill a dog.

Its leg went down, his head up. He tilted it as if listening. Then he turned. Faced them head-on. Growled.

Hal shot a look in their direction. "What is it, boy?"

Through the window, she saw Hal's gaze lock in on their hiding spot. She held her breath. Waited. He turned back. Moved inside. Came back, a rifle in his hands, phone to his ear.

Roger's phone vibrated in Matt's pocket, the vibration sounding as loud as a fire alarm in her brain. There was no way Matt could answer, and if he didn't, Hal would know something was wrong. He would come out. Start a search. Bring the dog.

Hal faced the house. "Roger's not answering. I'll take Zeus and check it out."

Stephen came to the door and ran his gaze over the area. "Leave Zeus with me."

"But I—"

"Don't need the dog as much as I do," Stephen finished for him. "Come, Zeus."

The dog bounded up the stairs and into the house.

Nicole let out a long breath.

Hal grumbled something and headed down the stairs to stomp across the yard.

Matt turned. Signaled for her to sit down and stay put. Then he mimed her staying there and him going after Hal. She didn't like Matt leaving her behind. Still, she knew he had to get to Hal before he found Roger and reported in.

She nodded.

He pressed a hand on her shoulder and disappeared

into the dark. In his absence, she didn't know which way to look—at the house or the direction Matt had taken. She couldn't see anything the way he headed and kept her focus on the house, where at least the light from inside shone into the black of night.

A biting wind penetrated her jacket. She tucked her legs up and circled them with her arms to stay warmer. She sat there, her mind racing.

Where were the deputies?

Surely it had been long enough since Matt called his father that they should have responded by now. But then, she could no longer determine the actual passing of time. Each second she sat there exposed, no protection, felt like an hour. Maybe longer.

A gunshot rang through the night, coming from the direction where Matt had gone.

No. No, God. No. Please don't let Matt have been shot.

She listened. Waited for a signal from him. Anything.

Silence, save for the sounds of Stephen and Zeus coming to the front door. She expected Stephen to bolt outside, but he held a phone to his ear. Was he trying to call Hal?

Likely. He started talking. She couldn't make out his words.

If he was talking to Hal, it meant Matt had been shot, right?

She had to go see. Just had to.

She climbed to her feet and turned her back on Stephen. She hated the feeling, but she could never let someone die if she could help them. She slipped as quietly as she could through the woods. If she made a sound, Hal would hear her and shoot. Or even Matt, if he was alive, could hear the sound and fire.

She slowed her footsteps. Planted them one at a time to ensure complete silence.

She stepped on a twig. It snapped and echoed through the night. She dove for cover behind a tree. Held her breath, waited and listened.

Nothing happened.

She peeked out.

Saw nothing aside from tree branches swaying in the strong wind.

She started to get up.

Suddenly a hand went around her mouth and fear took her down.

"Don't scream, honey," Matt told Nicole from behind her. "Fairhurst and Zeus are heading this way."

Matt released his hand from her mouth and got to his feet. He raised his rifle, his brain conflicted. He didn't want to shoot the dog, but if their lives depended on it he would have to. He'd aim for the hindquarters to ensure missing any vital organs. Now, Fairhurst was another thing altogether. Matt would follow his training. Tap two shots to the chest. He had to bring Fairhurst down before he got off a shot at them.

The moon broke through the clouds above and snow started falling softly on the field. Fairhurst moved across the ground, the dog by his side. If not for the danger, Matt would smile at the snowy scene.

The dog lifted his head and sniffed.

"What is it, boy?" Stephen asked. "You smell them?"

Matt was afraid he did and waited, his gun raised. He heard a car engine in the distance.

Fairhurst heard it, too, and spun. Tires soon rolled down the gravel driveway. A car door opened.

Yes, reinforcements.

"Let's move, boy." Fairhurst took off running toward the house.

Matt dug out the phone and texted his contact that he'd been communicating with since he'd left Nicole behind.

Leader headed your way. Armed and has a German shepherd.

He shoved the phone in his pocket and faced Nicole. "That's our reinforcements. They'll tranquilize the dog if they have to and arrest Fairhurst."

"And Hal?"

"He drew on me, and I had to shoot him. He was alive when I last saw him. I packed his wound with a bandanna and medics are on the way, too."

"So this is over?"

"Yes."

She threw her arms around his neck and started sobbing. He held her tightly, relishing the feel of her in his arms. The closeness. He hated that she was crying, but it was as much an adrenaline release as anything, and it gave him an excuse to keep her in his arms.

Her crying slowed, and when it subsided, she pulled back. "I thought we were going to die."

"Hey, now. I told you I had this, didn't I?" He tried to joke to lighten her stress.

"I should have trusted you."

"It's a tough position to be in. Instincts and adrenaline kick in. We don't think straight."

"But you did."

"I'm trained to do so," he said, but deep down he was shaken. Not for his own life, but for how close he came to losing her. One more minute and the dog and Fairhurst would've been barreling down on them, and he would've had to fire the rifle one more time.

He drew her close again.

"I thought I would lose you," she whispered against his neck. "And I hadn't told you."

"Told me what?"

"I'm in love with you."

Stunned, he rocked back on his haunches. "I had no idea it got that far for you, too."

"Too." Her eyes widened. "You mean you feel the same way?"

"Yes. I love you, too," he said. He still hadn't worked out in his mind how he could love her the way she deserved, though, and Emilie, too. They both needed his time, and he just didn't have that to give.

Her eyebrow arched. "You make it sound like a bad thing."

"It's not. You're amazing. Emilie's amazing, but I...I just can't do this now. You know that, right? I mean, my job and all."

Her smile faded. "Yeah, you mentioned that."

"And then I led you on. Kissing you when I shouldn't have. I'm sorry, I—" His phone buzzed, taking his attention. Seeing his contact's number, he answered. "Deputy McKade."

"Dog and suspect in custody. Mind taking us to the victim and his buddy?"

Yeah, Matt minded. He wanted to stay here and talk with Nicole, but this was his life. Law enforcement. It came first and always had to. "Head due south, and we'll be out in the yard waiting for you."

Matt stood and held out his hand. "Time to meet with the deputies who came to our rescue."

Nicole ignored his hand and got to her feet. She looked mad.

He deserved for her to be angry with him. He was no different than Harmon. Just when she started to care for him, he'd withdrawn. But what else could he do?

EIGHTEEN

Three hours later, fear once again wrapped its tentacles around Nicole, and she wanted to flee. The only thing keeping her from rushing out of the hospital where Grady waited to speak to her was Matt walking beside her down the hallway. Strong, tall, ready for battle again, he looked fierce, but he was vulnerable. She knew that, and despite the pain she felt from him choosing his job over her, she didn't like that he went out each and every day to face bad guys.

She glanced at his wrist. The medics had closed his wound with butterfly bandages, but it was still red and angry looking and would need stitches. Had to hurt like crazy, but if it did, he didn't mention it. Just like he didn't mention how she owed him her life. He was a quiet, strong man who didn't need praise. Now, Grady, he was another story. He'd craved affirmation.

Grady. What was she going to say to him? The closer they came to his room, the more she wanted to back away. But she had to talk to him. To hear his side of the story and see if he truly had been out for her best interests all along.

A tall, darkly handsome deputy stood outside the door.

"Seth." Matt greeted him and faced Nicole. "This is my cousin Seth."

"Is Grady under arrest?" she asked.

Matt nodded. "We still have a lot to sort out to determine official charges and jurisdiction, but at a minimum he violated his restraining order, and we can hold him on that."

She had to admit that she didn't like the thought of someone she'd once cared about going to prison. If it was up to her, she would make sure he didn't serve time for the restraining order violation, as he'd really tried to protect her. But if he'd been involved in other crimes, then so be it.

"Ready?" Matt asked.

"As long as you come with me."

He arched his eyebrow. "Are you sure?"

"Positive," she answered though she was still hurt by their earlier conversation.

"Then I'm right by your side." He pushed the door open.

She stepped into the room to see Grady lying in the bed, face pale, his eyes closed. His wrist was cuffed to the rail, sending a wave of shock down Nicole's body. She knew he'd broken the law but physically seeing the evidence hit home.

She stepped to his bed, and his eyes flashed open. That intense, cop glare took over until he recognized her, and his gaze softened. "I didn't think I'd see you again."

She still felt too vulnerable near him and backed up a few steps. "I need you to explain what happened. How you could get involved with men like Stephen Fairhurst."

He frowned. "I did it for you."

"Right, me. I'm not buying that, Grady."

"It was." He tried to sit up but winced and lay back. He reached for her.

Matt stepped closer, his hand out as if ready to protect her again.

Grady glared at Matt. "Still have your bodyguard, I see."

"And I'll be by her side until you're behind bars," Matt said.

Grady shifted his focus to her. "I won't hurt you, sweetheart. I never wanted to hurt you." He sighed out a long breath. "It's just—you were used to nice things. I wanted to provide them for you. So I took on some responsibilities for Stephen to earn extra money."

"According to Fairhurst, you took on criminal activities before you were even dating Nicole," Matt said.

Grady cringed. "Fine. It wasn't a big deal. Just some extra spending money."

"Engaging in any illegal activity is a big deal." Matt sounded disgusted with Grady. "Even more so for a police officer."

"I agree," Nicole said. "And I told you I didn't care about money and things, so don't try to blame me for that, either."

His eyes darkened as if he was getting mad, but then he took a long breath and let it out. "At first, I couldn't believe that, you know? I mean, what person doesn't want the best money can buy? I thought you were just trying to spare my feelings. But then I got to know you better and saw how deep your Christian convictions went, and I got worried."

She scoffed. "Since when did you start caring about that?"

"I don't. Not really." He ran his free hand over his face. "But I was worried if you found out about the kind of men I was involved with that you'd leave me. So I decided to quit." He frowned. "When I told them, they weren't having it. Said I knew too much, and they'd kill me before letting me quit. I didn't know what to do. Then you broke up with me."

"And now I'm even more glad I did."

"Yeah, I deserved it. There was a strain between us. My fault. I was trying to work through what to do with the firm, and I clammed up. It's just… I didn't want you to find out about them."

"I understand that, I guess, but you also got controlling."

"I had to, don't you see?" He managed to rise up on his elbow and locked gazes with her. "I was worried the firm might use you to keep me in line. I was afraid they might hurt you. I had to keep you home and know your every move to protect you."

She sighed. "You should just have told me."

"I would have if I thought it would bring us back together. But your moral compass is so strong, and you never deviate from it."

"You make it sound like that's a bad thing," Matt said. "When Nicole should be proud of it."

"Says her Boy Scout."

"If you plan to insult us like this, we're leaving," Nicole said.

"No, wait. I'm just trying to explain. I knew you would use my failure as another reason not to be with me."

"And so you hounded me."

"I wouldn't say hounded, but yeah. I wanted us to be together and told my lieutenant what I'd done. They offered me immunity to turn Stephen in, and I'd be free to be with you. That's why I called and tried to see you."

"And why were you following me? Putting a tracker on my car?"

He fell back on the bed. "I guess I got kinda obsessed with getting back together. It was all that mattered. I even let a few responsibilities at the firm slide."

"And they came after me for that."

"I didn't know that at first. You gotta believe me." He cast her a pleading look. "Not until I saw the knife on your counter. That's when I knew. Only then. And I wanted to help you, but you'd split. So I came here to keep an eye on you. To keep you safe. But I couldn't tell you I was here. You wouldn't believe me and would've gone running into danger. That's why I put the sugar in your tank. To keep you nearby." He shook his head. "When Stephen's crew showed up, though, I wished I hadn't. That you could've left and gotten as far from them as possible."

"You mean to keep them from shooting me."

"My fault again. One of Stephen's thugs found me watching the garage. He shot at you to prove a point. I took off. He came after me."

"And you killed him in the field," Matt said.

"It was self-defense, man. I just went on autopilot then. Grabbed his ID and bolted so I could warn you."

"And the guy's name?"

"Calvin Winters." Grady faced Nicole. "That's everything. You know the rest."

"The rest?" she said. "What about the future? If you go to prison, they have phones. Are you going to start calling me again? And when you get out, then what? Stalker time again?"

"I'll leave you alone."

"How can I be sure of that?"

"I'm giving you my word."

"I'm grateful to you for wanting to protect me from Stephen and his men, but forgive me if I don't trust your word."

"Fair enough. If you can't trust me, then I guess you'll just have to see by my actions, or lack of them."

Nicole fisted her hands but couldn't think of a single thing to say.

"In case you don't plan to follow through on this," Matt said, ice in his voice, "I'll be watching. If you come anywhere near Nicole or try to call her, you'll wish you hadn't."

Nicole loved how Matt was sticking up for her again. After their recent conversation, though, she knew he wouldn't be around to watch over her, and she and Emilie once again would be on their own.

Matt ground his teeth together as they stepped down the hallway. He should have questioned Harmon and told Nicole not to put herself through seeing him. Matt suspected she had no more closure than when she'd gone in.

He escorted her to his car and soon had them heading toward the ranch.

She swiveled in her seat. "Can you call Clem as soon as we get home to see if he'll pick up my car and work on it again?"

Home. She'd called the ranch home, and yet she wanted to talk to Clem about fixing her car and leaving town.

"With tomorrow being Christmas Eve," she continued, "I want to see if he can finish the repair or if I'll need Piper to come for me and Emilie."

"I'll call him," Matt said, and hated the words as he said them.

"You sound mad about doing it."

"Mad? No. I just… Why are you so eager to leave now that you don't need to go on the run?"

"I need to go home."

"Need to or want to?"

"Same difference."

"Is it?"

She sighed.

"Sorry. I'm just not ready for the two of you to leave."

She eyed him, her gaze sad and resigned. "But you're also not ready for us to stay."

"I…" he said but couldn't continue. He was no more ready for a relationship than he'd been several hours ago and there was no point in discussing it. "Is it okay if I let Emilie sit on a horse tomorrow before you go?"

"Yes."

"Do you want to join us?"

"Sit on a horse, no, but watch her, yes."

He thought about his days with the special little girl and wanted to do more than let her sit on the horse. He wanted to teach her how to ride. How to care for the horse. Maybe get her one of her own. Go riding together. Get her mother on one, too, and the three of them…

The three of them what? Would live in limbo until after the election? At that rate, he'd be single for life.

"Emilie will be so thankful," Nicole said. "And excited."

"She's really something, isn't she?"

"I like to think so."

"I do, too. My whole family does."

"She's really felt at home here, and I owe your mother and nana a big debt. They made a bad situation special for her. I'll never be able to repay them. You, too. I owe you my life. Thank you."

"They won't expect it and neither do I."

"You're a good man, Matt McKade. A very good man and you've fully restored my faith in men. Sure, there are guys like Grady out there. Too many of them, but I'm confident if I just keep my head on straight and my faith intact, I can spot them and won't make the same mistake again."

Matt thought about her with another man, and his heart clutched. He couldn't let her leave. Let her fall in love with another guy after she'd said she loved him. But what could he offer her?

While they'd waited for his father to pick them up at the cabin, she'd told Matt she was trusting God again. Had taken His hand, she'd said. But could he trust God to have his back, too? He didn't go in for holding God's hand, but maybe he should.

He hadn't been calm when they'd been abducted. At least not inwardly. He'd worried every step of the way. Not for himself, but for Nicole. The thought of her dying cut him to the quick.

How could he sit here and think he could let her leave?

She was more important than any job.

It was time to put aside his fear of failing as a sheriff, and trust in God's will and not let this amazing woman walk out of his life.

NINETEEN

Christmas Eve arrived, and the season's decorations were all around Matt. He stared out the foyer window at the wreaths and the lights on the railings. The big tree stood next to him. Christmas music played in the background, his family laughing as they constructed gingerbread houses at the dining room table. Even snow fell outside. A perfect day to end his worry and take the next step in his life. They had given their statements at the crime scene to the appropriate law enforcement agencies, their involvement with Harmon and Fairhurst was over and they could relax.

Emilie, her face covered in white icing, came running into the foyer and hugged his leg.

She looked up at him. "My house is done. Can I sit on the horsey now?"

"Absolutely."

She jumped up and down and reached for the door knob.

"Hold on." He smiled at her enthusiasm. "We need to get all bundled up. It's cold outside."

"Hurry," she said and grabbed her tiny boots sitting by much larger boots on a doormat, and that sight alone melted Matt's heart.

"We should ask your mom to come with us."

She frowned. "She's still afraid."

"Let's ask anyway."

Emilie ran into the dining room. "I'm gonna sit on a horsey. Come, too, Mommy."

Nicole looked up from the house she and Emilie had completed and nodded. "But first we need to get your face cleaned up."

"Aw," Emilie grumbled.

"Horses aren't fond of stickiness." Jed smiled at Emilie.

"'kay." She dropped her boots and took her mom's hand. "C'mon, Mommy. Hurry."

Nicole got to her feet and looked at Lexie with a grin. "See what you have to look forward to."

"I can't wait." Lexie pressed her hands on her belly. "And can only hope our child is as adorable."

"Um," Gavin said. "What if it's a boy?"

"Boys can be adorable, too." Lexie pinched Gavin's cheeks. "I mean, look at that face."

Gavin groaned as the family laughed.

Smiling, Matt shrugged into his jacket and planted his hat on his head.

Emilie soon came towing her mother into the space. She'd stopped to pick up her boots on the way and dropped onto the stairs. Nicole went to get Emilie's coat, but her daughter was so eager that she was about to put the wrong boot on the wrong foot.

Matt knelt by her and gently directed her to the right foot.

"Which horsey can I ride?" Her rapt expression was almost too much for Matt's heart to bear.

"Sit on," he corrected. "I have a surprise for you."

"A spuprise." Her eyes widened. "Really? Is it my own horsey?"

Matt laughed. "Sorry, sweetie. It's not that."

She frowned.

"Hey," Nicole said from behind them. "Remember we're leaving today, and it wouldn't make sense for you to have a horse."

Emilie's frown deepened. "Don't want to leave."

"I know, sweetie." Nicole helped Emilie to her feet and slipped her coat on. "It's been fun here, but we have to go back home."

"Why?"

"I have a job, and Aunt Piper is missing us."

"She can come here."

"That's a great idea," Matt said, as he was feeling guilty about not making his intentions clear yet, but he couldn't do so with his whole family nearby. "Why not spend Christmas with us? Piper can come, too. The more the merrier."

"Please, Mommy," Emilie pleaded.

Nicole frowned at him. "I'm sorry, sweetie. We need to go home today. But you can still sit on the horse."

Emilie kept frowning all the way through getting her mittens and hat on. More guilt piled on Matt's shoulders, and he hoped she would cheer up soon. He opened the door.

"Snow!" Emilie charged down the steps, and a sense of relief filled Matt.

"Oh, to be that young and let disappointments go that easily," Nicole said.

"I hate to think of you ever being disappointed again."

"Hey, that's life, right? But at least I have my priorities right now and know to turn to God when that happens."

"C'mon, Mommy," Emilie called from where she was sitting in the snow.

Nicole jogged down the steps, and Matt followed. She took Emilie's hand, and they both skipped through the snow. He hoped this wasn't a sign, that even after he declared his love, they would skip out of his life.

Nothing could compare to a life with these two. Nothing.

Nicole had been trying to put on a brave front for her daughter, but her heart was aching. She wanted to be with Matt and had prayed about it last night. It was clear to her that God was on board with them being together, but Matt hadn't seemed to get the message. And worse yet, he'd been in a great mood while her heart was breaking. But no matter what, she would put on a cheerful face for Emilie.

They stepped up to the barn, and Matt jogged ahead to open the big door. Beauty stood in the first stall, her head hanging over the gate. She whinnied, as did several of the other horses.

"Hey, girl." Matt walked up to her and patted her neck.

"I want to touch her," Emilie said.

Matt scooped her up. "Horses like when you stroke their neck and aren't as keen on having their faces petted. Can you do that?"

Emilie nodded, her expression so serious, Nicole had to smile. Matt lifted her up to sit on the half door. She touched Beauty's neck tentatively at first, then smiled and rubbed. "I like her."

"She likes you, too."

"Is this my spuprise?" she asked.

"No, would you like to see it?"

"Yes, please."

Nicole was so proud of her daughter right now. She was overly excited and yet she remembered her manners.

As Matt lifted her, Emilie flung her arms around his neck. Nicole's heart melted. She wanted to be there, too. The three of them. Forever.

"It's this way." He turned and reached out for Nicole's hand.

At the touch of his fingers, her heart soared, and she had to work hard to tamp down her feelings before she started crying. He led her to the last stall. Nicole strained to see the surprise, but the stall seemed to be empty. What in the world was his surprise? She was as eager as Emilie to see it.

He released Nicole's hand and opened the gate. In the back of the stall, a buckskin pony stood there, looking at them.

"He's my size," Emilie exclaimed and rushed toward the pony, who came to the top of her head.

"She," Matt corrected. "Her name is Butterscotch."

"Where did you get her?" Nicole asked.

"Borrowed her from our neighbors. They've had her for years. Got her when their kids were young, but they're way too big for her now."

"She's so cute." Nicole stepped into the stall and stroked the pony's neck.

"Your fear of horses doesn't extend to ponies, then," he said.

"Are you kidding?" She chuckled. "What's to be afraid of?"

"I want up," Emilie cried out, startling the pony.

"First," Matt said. "You need to learn to be calmer around horses or you'll scare them."

Emilie nodded, the same serious look on her face that Nicole often saw in church during the message.

"I want up," she whispered, but her eyes still sparkled.

"Then let's saddle her up and you can."

Emilie started to dance, then quickly stopped. "Don't want to scare her."

"First a thick pad," he said.

"Is the pony cold?" Emilie asked.

Matt chuckled. "No, it absorbs sweat and cushions the saddle. All in all, it makes it comfier for the horse to wear the saddle."

He stepped away to grab a pad and miniature saddle from a stand in the corner. He put the covering on the pony's back, then set the saddle on top. He squatted to grab the strap. "This's called a cinch, and it holds the saddle to keep it from falling off and taking you with it."

He tightened the strap and stood.

"Ready." Emilie lifted her arms.

"Not quite yet. She needs a bit and reins."

He grabbed a bridle and put it on the horse. Emilie was about to lose patience.

Nicole knelt next to her daughter. "She's almost ready for you."

Emilie patted Butterscotch's neck. "I love her, Mommy, and she loves me."

"I know, sweetie."

Matt finished his work. "One last thing."

Emilie sighed.

"It's another surprise."

Her frown disappeared.

He grabbed a box from the aisle and handed it to her. "An early Christmas present."

"Present!" she squealed and lifted the lid.

Nicole bent over her daughter to see the cutest red cowboy hat nestled in the box.

"A hat," she exclaimed and ripped off her stocking cap to put it on. "Oh, Mommy, boots, too."

She jerked a pair of matching red boots from the box and dropped to her bottom. Nicole let her daughter take off her other boots while she looked up at Matt.

He stared at Emilie with such affection and love, Nicole's heart melted. She got to her feet and kissed him on the cheek.

"Thank you," she said. "That was so thoughtful."

A red blush stole up his neck. "I figured Emilie would like them. Mom and Nana picked them out, though."

"They're perfect."

Emilie started to pull on the first boot.

"Other foot, sweetie," Nicole called out.

She stood, and Nicole had never seen a more adorable sight.

"Ready." She beamed from under the hat, her precious blond curls softly framing her face.

Matt scooped her up and set her in the saddle. "Put your feet in the stirrups."

He helped her get them in place and handed her the reins. "There's a lot I have to teach you about using these, but for now, just sit here and enjoy it."

He kept a hand on the pony but stood back a little, allowing Nicole to see her daughter's pure joy. Matt was amazing with her. Patient. Loving. Kind.

Oh, how Nicole wished Matt could be in Emilie's life for good.

Her heart breaking, Nicole snapped a few pictures with Matt's phone, and they stood there, the three of them, as time ticked by.

Once Emilie had finally had her fill, she wiggled to get down.

Matt set her on the straw.

"Want to go back to the house," she said. "And show everyone my hat and boots."

Matt nodded. "Normally I'd teach you how to untack Butterscotch and take care of her, but I'll come back and do it later. For now, I'll just take out the bit and loosen the cinch so the pony can breathe."

Emilie nodded and adjusted her hat, then planted a hand on her hip and preened.

Matt chuckled and turned to Nicole. "She looks great in her hat and boots. I thought it would be good for her to have something horse related."

"Thank you."

"You know," he continued, "our neighbors don't have much use for Butterscotch anymore, and they said they'd sell her to me."

Nicole spun to face him. "There'd be no point in that."

"There would be if you stayed."

"You mean for Christmas?"

"No." He met and held her gaze. "I mean forever."

"What are you saying?"

He took her hand and drew her close. "I'm saying I'm crazy in love with you, and I want us to see where this goes between us. To do that, I'd need you here in Lost Creek."

"But I…" She didn't know what to say.

He cupped the side of her face. "We have schools here, too. They need teachers all the time."

"But your run for sheriff? The job? You thought we'd be in the way."

"I was a fool. I love you so much and living like that when I could have you and Emilie in my life would be the dumbest thing I could ever do." He circled his arms around her waist and pulled her closer. "Will you and Emilie stay in Lost Creek?"

"Yes!" Emilie called out.

"You see," he said. "Emilie agrees."

"I don't know." Nicole bit her lip.

He frowned. "What do you have to lose by staying and giving us a chance?"

She honestly didn't know. She shrugged.

"Then what do you have to lose by going?"

"Everything." The word came out involuntarily, and the future was suddenly clear to Nicole. "Well, you heard Emilie. We'll be staying."

"Yippee," Emilie shouted. "Oops. Scared Butterscotch. Sorry, Butterscotch."

Matt laughed and lowered his head to kiss Nicole.

"I love you, too," she said before his lips crashed down on hers.

He kissed her until she was breathless.

She felt a tug on her pant leg. "C'mon, Mommy. Haveta show them my boots and hat."

Matt released Nicole and scooped Emilie up into his arms. They looked quite the pair, with their cowboy hats. Emilie planted her hands on the side of Matt's face, and Nicole knew she planned to ask a big question or maybe declare her own love for Matt.

"Will you be my daddy?" she asked.

Matt seemed shocked at first, but love poured from his eyes. "You know I will."

Emilie's pudgy arms went around his neck, and she clung tight, knocking her hat off. Nicole picked it up, and when she stood back up, she saw Matt's eyes were bright with tears.

He cleared his throat. "Time to show off your hat and boots, princess."

Nicole put the hat on her daughter's head, and holding

Matt's hand, they strolled up to the house. In the foyer, Emilie squirmed down.

She ran into the dining room and posed with her hands on her hips. "I have a hat and boots, and I'm gonna have my own pony."

His family looked up, big questions in their expressions, and Nicole had a moment's concern.

"And Matt is going to be my daddy," Emilie added. "He said so."

A look of understanding traveled around the table, and the family burst out in applause and congratulations.

Matt slid his arm around Nicole's waist. "Welcome to the McKade family, honey. It's clear they love you as much as I do."

"I'm so touched."

"And I feel incredibly blessed." He pulled her close to him and placed a kiss on her head. "You agreeing to give us a chance is like a Christmas blessing."

"For me, too." She smiled up at this most incredible man who God put in her life. "Faith brought us together, and I know it will keep us together. Now and forever."

* * * * *

If you enjoyed this story, don't miss the exciting
first installments in Susan Sleeman's
McKade Law miniseries:

Rodeo Standoff
Holiday Secrets

Find more great reads at www.LoveInspired.com

Dear Reader,

Thank you for reading *Christmas Hideout*. I have loved every moment of writing about the McKade family, and I hope you have enjoyed getting to know them in the first three books of the miniseries. In this story, both Nicole and Matt struggle with trusting God with their futures. They worry about the unseen and need to realize that God can see into the future, that they can take heart, that though their future may not be what they expected or planned for, He always promises to work things for our good. If you struggle with the same thing, I hope reading about how Nicole and Matt overcome their issues helps you cope with your own.

If you'd like to learn more about the McKade Law miniseries or my other books, please stop by my website at *www.susansleeman.com*. I also love hearing from readers, so please contact me via email, susan@susansleeman.com, on my Facebook page, www.facebook.com/SusanSleeman-Books, or write to me c/o Love Inspired, HarperCollins, 24th Floor, 195 Broadway, New York, NY 10007.

Susan Sleeman

Get 4 FREE REWARDS!

We'll send you 2 FREE Books <u>plus</u> 2 FREE Mystery Gifts.

TEXAS RANGER SHOWDOWN
Margaret Daley

SECRET PAST
SHAREE STOVER

Love Inspired® Suspense books feature Christian characters facing challenges to their faith... and lives.

FREE
Value Over
$20

SPECIAL EXCERPT FROM

Robin Hardy may be the only one who can help former spy Toby Potter—but she can't remember her past with him or who is trying to kill her.

Read on for a sneak preview of
Holiday Amnesia *by Lynette Eason,*
the next book in the Wrangler's Corner series,
available in December 2018 from
Love Inspired Suspense.

Toby Potter watched the flames shoot toward the sky as he raced toward the building. "Robin!"

Sirens screamed closer. Toby had been on his way home when he'd spotted Robin's car in the parking lot of the lab. Ever since Robin had discovered his deception—orders to get close to her and figure out what was going on in the lab—she'd kept him at arm's length, her narrow-eyed stare hot enough to singe his eyebrows if he dare try to get too close.

Tonight, he'd planned to apologize profusely—again—and ask if there was anything he could do to earn her trust back. Only to pull into the parking lot, be greeted by the loud boom and watch flames shoot out of the window near the front door.

Heart pounding, Toby scanned the front door and rushed forward only to be forced back by the intense heat. Smoke billowed toward the dark night sky while the fire grew hotter and bigger. Mini explosions followed. Chemicals.

"Robin!"

Toby jumped into his truck and drove around to the back only to find it not much better, although it did seem to be more smoke than flames. Robin was in that building, and he was afraid he'd failed to protect her. Big-time.

Toby parked near the tree line in case more explosions were coming.

At the back door, he grasped the handle and pulled. Locked. Of course. Using both fists, he pounded on the glass-and-metal door. "Robin!"

Another explosion from inside rocked Toby back, but he was able to keep his feet under him. He figured the blast was on the other end of the building—where he knew Robin's station was. If she was anywhere near that station, there was no way she was still alive. "No, please no," he whispered. No one was around to hear him, but maybe God was listening.

Don't miss
Holiday Amnesia *by Lynette Eason,*
available December 2018 wherever
Love Inspired® Suspense books and ebooks are sold.

www.LoveInspired.com